Alexander Oakey

Home grounds

Alexander Oakey

Home grounds

ISBN/EAN: 9783337185275

Printed in Europe, USA, Canada, Australia, Japan

Cover: Foto ©Andreas Hilbeck / pixelio.de

More available books at **www.hansebooks.com**

Oakey and Jones, Architects.

Entrance Gate.

Appletons' Home Books.

HOME GROUNDS.

BY
ALEXANDER F. OAKEY,
AUTHOR OF "BUILDING A HOME."

NEW YORK:
D. APPLETON AND COMPANY,
1, 3, AND 5 BOND STREET.
1881.

CONTENTS.

HOME GROUNDS.

I.

GENERAL ARRANGEMENT OF GROUNDS.

"Strength may wield the ponderous spade,
    May turn the clod, and wheel the compost home;
    But elegance, chief grace, the garden shows,
    And most attractive is the fair result
    Of thought, the creature of a polished mind."—Cowper.

THE average human being first devotes his energies to acquiring his three daily meals, what he considers necessary raiment, and what he considers a fair lodging; but, when born to these necessities or when supplied with the means of providing them, he devotes his leisure to seeking what he considers enjoyment. It is in this search that his temper, his taste, and his aspirations show themselves, and by nothing more than by what he has done or left undone in improving and beautifying his immediate surroundings. Who can not fairly judge of the sanitary, intellectual, and moral status of a community or of a private dwelling by its outward conditions? The straggling squalor of the outskirts of cities is much more than sensually shocking in its analogy to the souls who are content with such surroundings. In short, where no prospect pleases, it is hardly to be wondered at if man is vile. It is futile to preach against alcohol to a man who finds in it a relief from the hideousness of his daily life. Our parks have already afforded a respite from the exigencies that largely support the rum-shops; but, until landscape gardening in its broadest sense is recognized as a constant necessity, we shall hardly do more than better the physical condition of a few people here and there in our large towns. In proof of this assertion—the constant efforts of philanthropists in sending poor children away from the cities with satisfactory results—without sentimentality, it is not too much to say that in a tour of our tenement-house districts, we shall find the happiest and most respectable families to be those who have a well-cared-for box of plants in their window. In short, he who has no love of nature lacks at least one quality of a man.

From all this it would seem that the duty of beautifying one's home is not altogether a selfish matter. Even a tastefully ordered backyard in a city will in time influence the standard of cleanliness and sightliness of the neighboring inclosures, rivalry among housewives, if no higher sentiment, often transforming in a few years a row of dreary garbage pens into trimly kept grass plots, where nothing more unsightly is ever permitted to appear than the fluttering forms of suspended underwear drying in the sun.

One of the advantages of a suburban home, with an acre or more of ground surrounding the house, is that even this washing-day spectacle can be concealed from the inmates of the house and from the neighbors.

The first province of landscape gardening is to abate nuisances of every kind and degree. With this object, to take all possible sanitary precautions in drainage, in nature of soil, and in character and extent of vegetation, natural advantages should be made available, and injurious changes, that often in time alter the conditions that constitute desirable or undesirable sites on land that is uncared for, should be considered. Of course, the most thorough and scientific precautions may be nullified by the carelessness of near neighbors, especially if their grounds are so relatively placed as to drain through. For the nuisance of noxious odors arising from neighboring pig-pens, oil or soap factories, there is no cure but a legal process or a removal to windward; but the nuisance of unsightly

or disgusting objects can always be met by judicious
planting, and thus it is in the power of every man, whose
house does not cover his whole lot, to make what space
is left more or less delightful, by the expenditure of
thought, directed by special knowledge, good taste, and
assisted in realization by more or less money, according
to the natural advantages or the peculiar disadvantages
existing.

Although we propose in the following pages to suggest what special knowledge is necessary, and how it can
be attained, and to give a few instructions that may be
found sufficient for the successful treatment of a few
acres, we shall avoid scientific disquisition, and as far as
possible all technicalities which would properly be included in any complete treatise on landscape gardening.

Our object is to discuss what can and ought to be
done to make our external home surroundings attractive
and healthful, and, by implication, to define what should
not be attempted within narrow boundaries. We have
seen more than one city yard treated as a miniature park,
with lake and grove, lawn and terrace, and, though no
pains were spared, the effect was only that of elaborate
toys, of one of which the owner said, "My wife calls that
place her landscape garden, but I call it a grave for
greenbacks."

Any garden or park is apt to be a mere "grave for
greenbacks" if the natural features are utterly disre-
garded in the scheme of improvement adopted. Lakes,

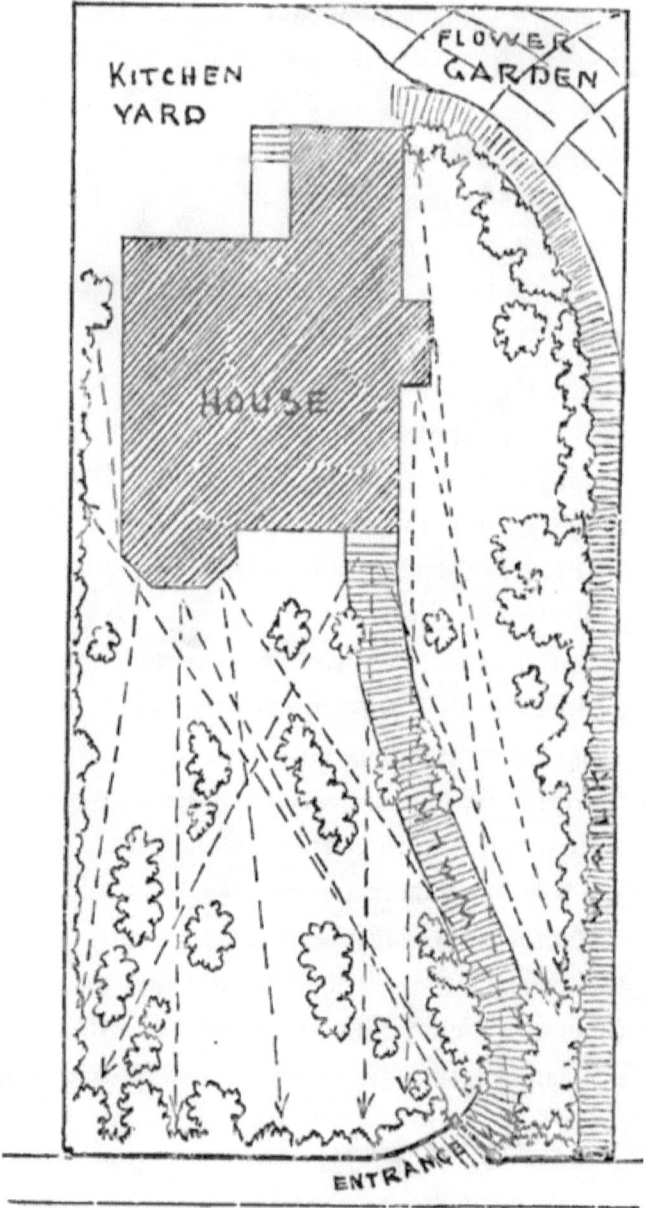

STREET

FIG. 1.

waterfalls, caverns, and dense woodlands can be manufactured at great expense, but the investor is likely to die before Nature has time to accomplish the desired effect, if, indeed, she ever can make artifice her own. In contradistinction to this manufacturing of freaks of Nature, there is the professedly artificial garden, with its terraces, its symmetrically disposed flower-beds in the shape of hearts, lyres, and what not, its geometric plan of walks, and its clipped hedges and trees in formal array. Although this treatment is not attractive to a lover of nature, there are undoubtedly conditions under which it can be very magnificent, especially if it accompanies a stately marble villa of ample proportions. However we may prefer natural beauties in our home surroundings, we can not be insensible to the traditional charm that pervades the surroundings of an old château. The peacock that still sweeps the moss-grown pavement of the terrace with his gorgeous train is a reminder of the brocaded and powdered duchesses whose brilliant presence once enhanced the costly grandeur of the effect. The traditional charm is what we can not manufacture if we would, and it seems as if marble terraces and formal avenues adorned with statues, at least as home surroundings, were as much out of date as bagwig and ruffles and class privileges. So that we shall content ourselves with this allusion to artificial gardening, assuming that a discussion of the useful and natural art of landscape gardening is more likely to interest and benefit our readers.

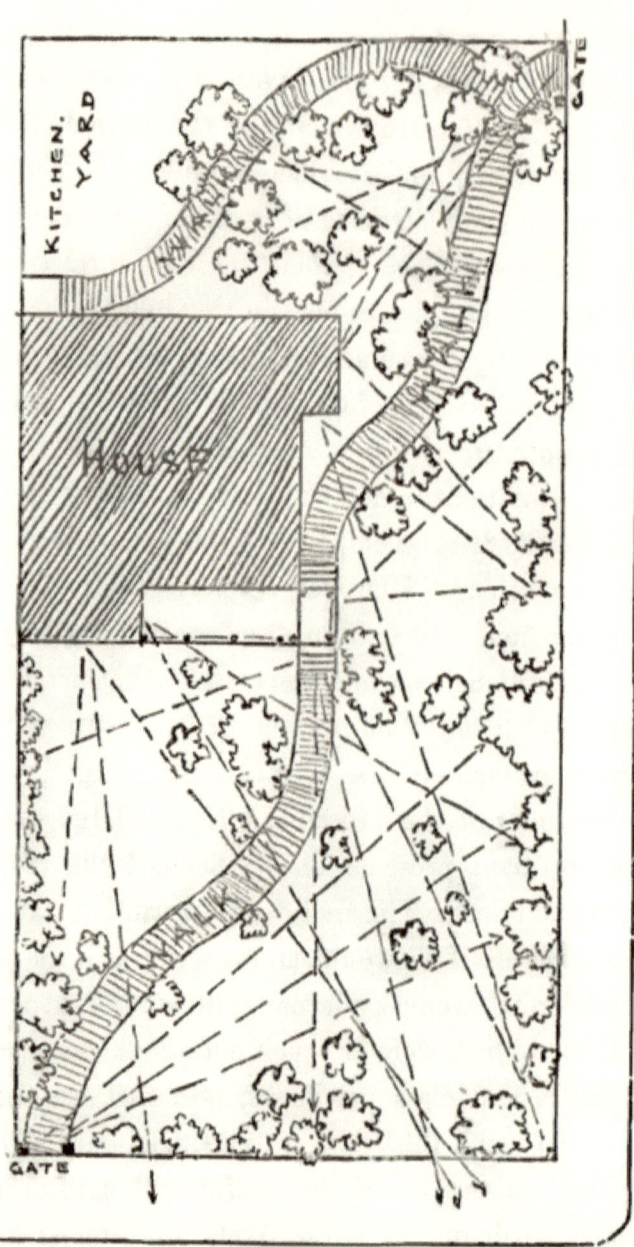

FIG. 2.

The question of what to do in improving and beautifying home grounds is always primarily a question of
what not to do. We are acquainted with one gentleman
who, before consulting his landscape gardener, and in
order to give him a fair chance to display his skill, spent
what money was necessary to reduce his entire garden to
a dead level, obliterating all natural formations and
clearing away all existing vegetation, and it is hardly
necessary to say that his grounds have never outgrown
the effects of his vandalism. Of course, in any scheme
of gardening, more or less grading has to be done, but it
is an object to do as little as possible. The grounds should
be laid out, at least on paper, before the house is built,
so that all superfluous earth from the excavations may be
dumped, once and for all, where it is to remain. In cases
where the house is an already established fact, we must
make the best of what is too often an ill-considered disposition, and try to counteract the mistake by ingenious
contrivance.

It may be unqualifiedly asserted that on limited
grounds, such as are usual in the suburbs, the house
should never occupy a central position, but should always
be nearer one end, and much nearer one side of the lot,
thus acting as a screen for the kitchen yard, kitchen
garden, and such necessary but uninteresting provisions
as there may be, when viewed from the grounds, as
shown in Fig. 1; and of course the living-rooms should
command a view of the grounds, while the kitchen offices

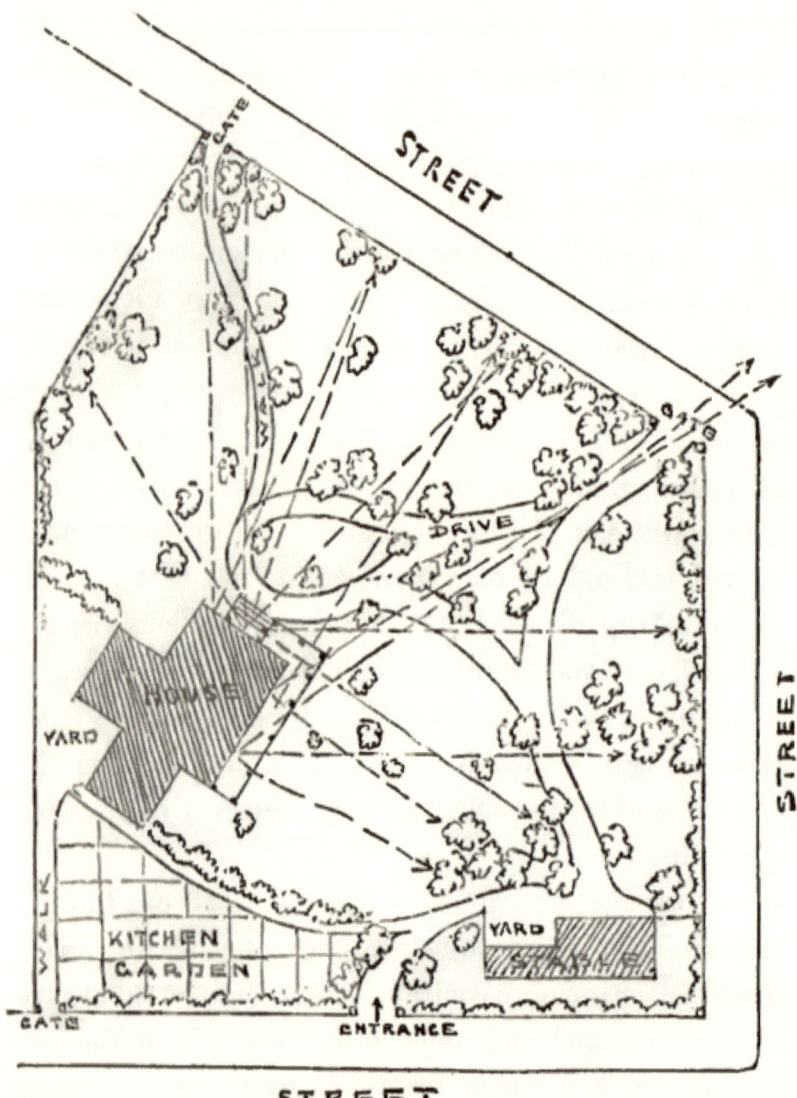

FIG. 3.

open upon the more limited area. This disposition can
always be realized in grounds of whatever general form,
whether they are bounded by adjoining property and one

street, by adjoining property and two streets, three
streets, or are completely isolated. Figs. 1, 2, 3, 4, and
5 are illustrations of existing grounds in different locali-

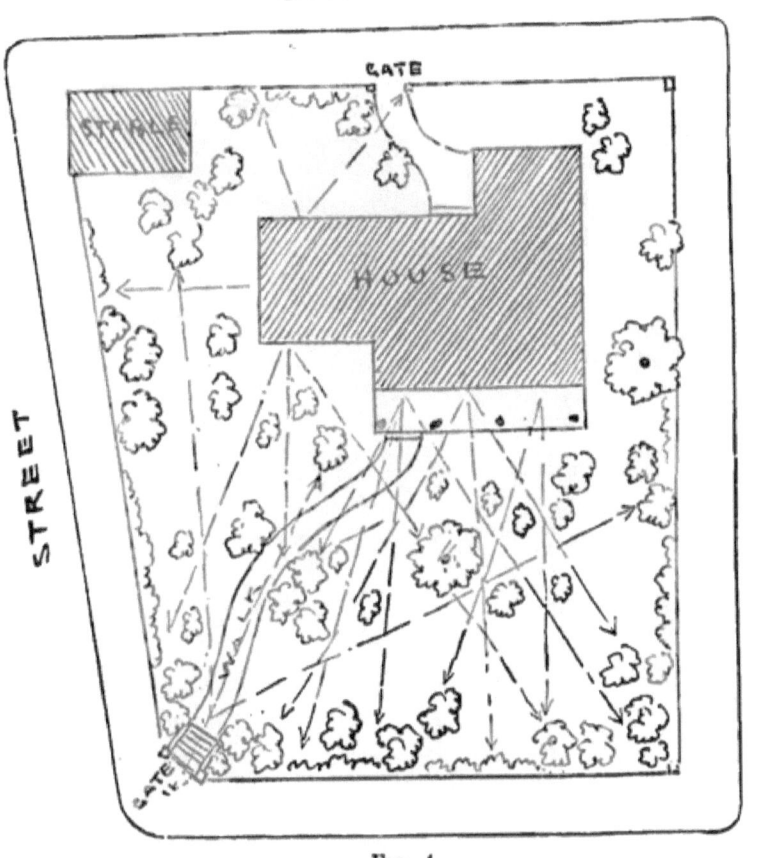

FIG. 4.

ties, all displaying the disposition of the buildings upon
which we are inclined to insist as the first element of
success in laying out small home grounds. Fig. 5 is also
an existing garden which, though commanding only one

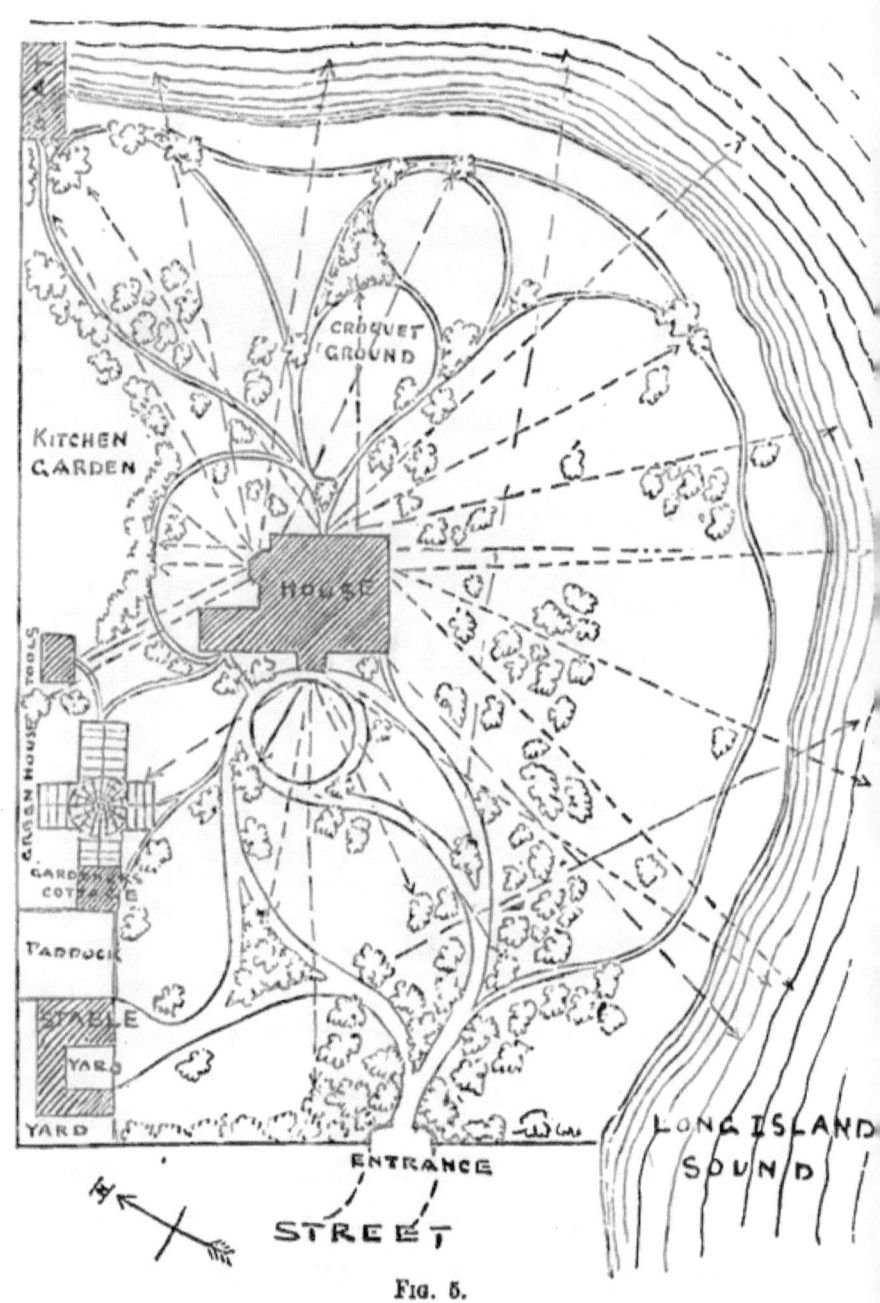

Fig. 5.

street, adjoins other property only on the north, and is
bounded by Long Island Sound on the south and east.
From these instances, to which we shall refer from time
to time, may be derived all necessary illustrations for our
discussion, as they are sufficiently various, in general plan
and in detail, to cover all probable requirements of small
home grounds.

Natural advantages may be classed under three heads:
Geological advantages, those that consist in the nature of
the ground itself; topographical advantages, those that
consist in the formation of the ground as to depressions
and elevations; and botanical advantages, those consist-
ing in the nature and extent of existing vegetation.

The best ground for successful gardening is that
which is underlaid with gravel beds, because the gravel
forms a natural drain for the top soil; but, where no such
natural drains exist, the most successful gardening can
only be accomplished after a thorough system of subsoil
drainage has been laid.   This is accomplished with
ordinary field drain tile, laid with the necessary fall to
carry off water—the courses of tile being about ten to
twenty feet apart, and not less than four feet below the
surface.   In small grounds the operation is not an expensive one, but it must be performed by competent
persons to be effective.   There are many causes of
stoppage to be guarded against, such as streaks of quick-
sand; and where these occur the tile must be packed
with straw and gravel.   These drainage precautions are

especially necessary to insure the health of fruit-trees as well as all half-hardy trees and shrubs, while all hardy vegetation will be much improved by it.

The line can not always be distinctly drawn between geological and topographical features, especially where the whole property is underlaid with rock which crops out here and there as features of the surface. Such a site renders subsoil drainage more than ordinarily necessary, because the ground in such cases is only the accumulation of centuries, filling a valley between two hills or mountains of rock, and must be permeated with fissures, which, if the ground is not level, will prove their existence by springs trickling out at various points down the slope.

If we are in search of water supply, we may determine

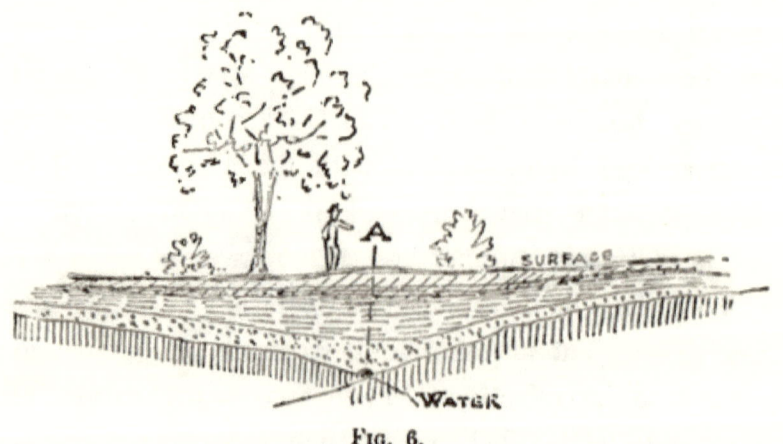

Fig. 6.

where our well should be sunk by boring down at several points on the boundaries of the property, and again at a

few spots within the inclosure, noting the nature and
direction of the strata or layers, and, if we can discover
that there is a depression or dip from two or more directions toward a common center, we can with confidence
sink our well at this point, which can readily be determined by measurement when the inclination of the strata
or layers has been found, as indicated in Fig. 6. The
existence of a brook or a pond on a small property is
generally undesirable, especially the pond. A running
brook may, on the other hand, be made very serviceable,
not as an attractive feature, but as a practical advantage,
in additional water supply at least for washing purposes,
or as a natural drain: in fact, both purposes may be
served if the drain enters below the point at which the
water is drawn; but, in any case, the brook should be
walled up on each side, all decaying vegetation removed
from the bed, and coarse gravel substituted. The brook
should then be covered with a brick arch or with flag-
ging, and with two or three feet of earth. In this way
no annoyance from dampness or mosquitoes will be felt,
while the brook will still perform all the service required
of it better than if subject to all sorts of disturbance.
Ponds only breed fevers, mosquitoes, and accidents to
children, and should, if stagnant, be drained off and
filled in. If not stagnant, they should be made by filling
and walling to form part of the brook as already described.

In small grounds, strongly marked topographical features are not desirable, but a rolling surface or a general slope extending over the whole area is much more advantageous than a dead level, on which it is generally necessary to do some grading to vary the monotony. This can sometimes be best accomplished by procuring a few large bowlders, if the neighborhood affords such, and by leaving some portions of them exposed in banking the earth about them, and grading off in a gradual slope to the surrounding level. It is hardly necessary to suggest that such a feature should not occupy a central position, but should rather mark the termination of a strip of lawn through a vista of trees and shrubbery.

If the general slope of the property is very steep, as in one instance we know of, where the fall is twelve feet in forty feet, it becomes necessary to cut off the top of the slope, and deposit it below in order to make the grade less abrupt, as in heavy rains the surface wash would otherwise make havoc with any improvements we might undertake. We are fortunate in such extreme cases if the slope is from the rear to the front of the site, and not the reverse, as in the instance we mention, where the public road now occupies a level four feet higher than the highest point in the garden, and the necessary precautions to sustain the sidewalk and to drain the road without injuring the garden, together with the entrance steps, have been a very costly matter.

Botanical advantages mainly consist in the existence of shade-trees, of such sort and in such stages of growth and in such relative positions, that we can include them in our schemes of improvement; nothing that the landscape gardener can do, with any amount of money at command, will compensate for a few broad-spreading, healthy trees rising out of a rich turf. We can supply a variety of ornamental shrubbery, vines, and flowers, and can dispose them tastefully over our lawns, and can accomplish any effect within the scope of these accessories at short notice; but time only can accomplish the beauties that are imparted by shade-trees, which require little assistance from the landscape gardener to make a garden beautiful.

There are some sorts of trees that should be cut down, however luxuriant and venerable, if we wish to succeed with our lawn and with all other planting. These are the black-walnut and the butternut, both of which destroy, more or less, all proximate vegetation.

Again, there are trees that have a disagreeable odor, such as the ailantus, and this also sends up shoots at great distances, so that one is by no means certain that it is gone when cut down, or even uprooted. In all probability we shall from time to time recognize an offspring trying to assert itself elsewhere on the place, and it grows so rapidly that these must be immediately dug out, in all directions, with their shoots, or we shall have the work to do over again.

Many others less objectionable, and many beautiful trees, such as the silver birch, have this faculty of acquiring a family circle, and are often valuable in forming a thicket to plant out an undesirable view, or produce a dense effect of planting. We shall return presently to the discussion of trees and planting when we have prepared our walks, lawns. and driveways, and disposed of the practical considerations involved.

II

WALKS AND DRIVES.

"He gains all points who pleasingly confounds
Surprises, varies, and conceals the bounds.
Calls in the country, catches opening glades,
Joins willing woods, and varies shades from shades;
Now breaks, or now directs, the intending lines;
Paints as you plant, and, as you work, designs."

THE driveway does not usually play an important part in grounds of small extent, and even when horses are kept, unless the house is at least fifty feet from the street, a driveway is unnecessary, and occupies too much valuable space, besides requiring constant care to keep it in proper condition. Of course, in grounds of even two acres a driveway becomes a necessity, and can be made a very graceful feature, affording an agreeable contrast to the lawns in its windings among the shrubbery. If we have a driveway, however small the grounds, let it be sufficiently wide to be really serviceable and look hospitable. Few things give a meaner expression to a place than narrow drives and walks. A drive should never be less than twelve feet wide, and a walk should at least be six feet wide, though more than nine feet is generally wider than is needed for private grounds. We all know that in dry weather it is pleasanter to walk upon the turf than upon any path ; but some paths must be provided to prevent tracks being worn in the turf on the lines of the most constant communication, besides the necessity of having a dry footing when the dew or recent rains have made the grass wet. We would not by any means advocate cutting up a small place with walks into grass plots and flower beds in order to provide a sufficiently long "constitutional" in wet weather; on the contrary, we believe that the less space we devote to walks and drives, the more effective our garden will be, and the less trouble and time will be required to keep it in order. Driveways and paths, being primarily roads to and from the house, must necessarily terminate at one or more of the entrances provided, unless they are planned merely to touch at the entrances at some point of their curve, so as to lead away from the house in opposite directions ; and this arrangement is the most obviously convenient for driveways, in order to admit of a carriage being driven round, instead of turning in a limited space. Practical considerations should, of course, govern the planning of paths and driveways as absolutely as they should the planning of a house; but there are so many ways of doing anything and everything with the same general results, that we may point out a few faults to be avoided, and a few virtues to be assumed, in this apparently simple undertak-

3

ing, the mention of which may assist the unqualified
experimenter.

Although our roads must all, sooner or later, in their
meanderings lead to the house, the less gravel surface
there is immediately about the house, the better. A
driveway or a path that leads up to, and again away from,
the house on a curve should be planned on as sharp a
curve as is practicable and effective, because the gravel
surface reflects the light and heat, making the house on
that side less comfortable in summer, not to mention the
dust that must rise from the best-made gravel road in dry
weather. A house set on the greensward is a much
more attractive and picturesque object than one, equally
elegant in proportion and detail, set on a desert of gravel.
It is a common disposition to have a path leading round
close to the house, from the front door to the back, leaving only a mere strip of turf next the building, and this
much encumbered with flower beds. We have never
been able to comprehend the advantages of this treatment, though we have often guessed the reasons that
have prompted its adoption. Where there is only one
gateway to a place, and that directly opposite the main-
entrance door, it is easy to see that the shortest road from
the gate to the back door will soon become marked if no
path is provided; but in such cases the difficulty lies at the
gate, which without appreciable inconvenience could be
opened fifteen or twenty feet farther on in one or other
direction, so that we could lay out our paths to the main

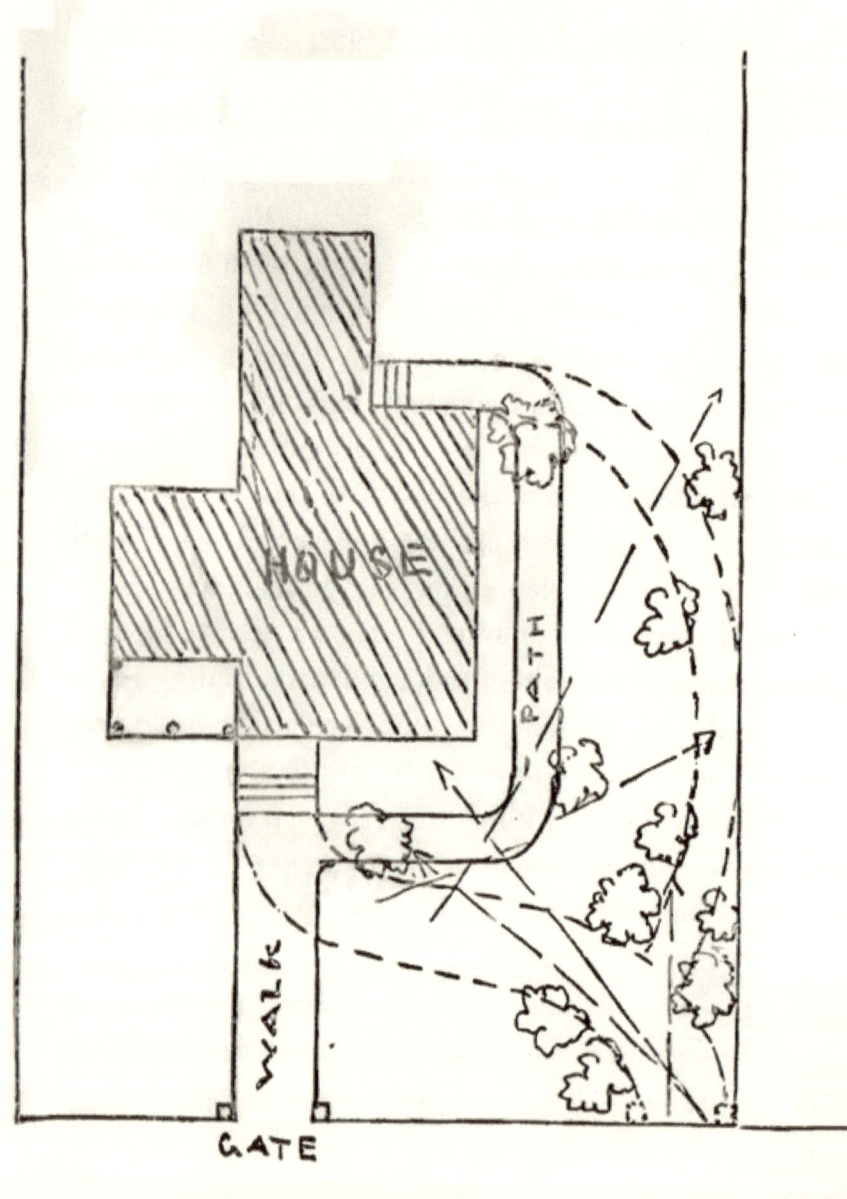

Fig. 7.

entrance and to the back entrance in two graceful curves coinciding at, and growing from, the gateway, and leaving the turf directly about the house undisturbed. The usual method and that we propose as a substitute are suggested in Fig. 7.

The position of the house in the first place, and of the entrance gate or gates in the second, and the relative positions of both, are the controlling principles in the plan of any garden. If these are not carefully studied and happily arranged, our garden is a failure from the start; while, on the other hand, it is comparatively easy to achieve effective results on a well-digested plan. This plan in a small place where the house already exists may consist of merely two or three lines where our paths are to be made, but it must be remembered that these lines divide our place into three or more parts, and that we shall find the form of these parts, whether good or bad, governing everything we may attempt in planting. The object of a path in a pleasure-ground is not only to get from one point to another dry shod, but to do so agreeably; and for this reason, although a straight line is the shortest distance between two points, we avoid setting out our places like a checker-board, and add something to the length of our paths, in order to give them a less business-like, direct expression, and consequently a more graceful one. For all this, very little, if anything, is gained by arbitrarily changing the general direction of a path or road. If the fundamental idea of its being is to get to a certain place, it

will be found most effective to lay it out with that place
in view with an easy sweep, the curve being sufficient to
prevent the whole distance from being seen at a glance.
To a certain degree, deception as to the extent of grounds
is not only legitimate but often necessary; the degree is
determined by the point at which the deception is obvious.
We want to realize in our garden as many and as charming natural effects as we can, and with this object we are
certainly committing no fraud if we conceal our back
fence, or if we curve our paths here and there sufficiently
to leave the question of the length of their wanderings
among the shrubbery undetermined.

Paths are often a great resource in solving difficult
problems of general effect. In small gardens it is usually
necessary to avoid all expensive preparation, and to
achieve creditable results with as little disturbance as
possible; if there exist any very marked irregularities on
the surface, we would generally prefer to modify them
by grading, which is an expensive matter, as we may do
a great deal of digging and carrying without making
much impression on the existing levels, so that we are
often glad to separate the strong contrast of a sudden
change of level by skirting it with a path which enables
us to have our lawn on one side trimly kept and level,
while on the other a steep bank, covered with a thicket of
shrubbery, becomes very effective without being in direct
opposition to our velvet lawn. Another advantage in
this arrangement is the apparently greater height of the

trees we may plant on the higher ground, as their
stems are concealed by the shrubbery on the bank.

The necessary differences between the treatment of
large grounds or private parks and small grounds or
gardens do not seem to be fully appreciated. There are
many effects and practical advantages peculiar to each
scale of operations, and while, as we have already said,
it is not only legitimate, but desirable, to adopt such a
plan and details for a small garden as shall, at all events,
prevent a correct estimate of its extent being readily
made, any attempt to give it the air of an extended park
must always end in a miniature treatment, which will be
at once accepted as a confession of lack of space. A
number of paths leading in all directions leave so little
lawn in small grounds, that after looking in vain for some
expanse of turf we realize that the paths really lead nowhere, and that they have merely been laid out to de-
ceive us, while they so confuse and parcel out the place
in small grass plots that little space is left to compensate
for our disappointment.

The first expression to aim at in landscape gardening
is simplicity. Grounds should look as much as possible as
if no great study had been spent upon them, as if they
could not well be otherwise than as they are, and this
effect can only be realized by great study; that is, after
the ground has been expertly examined almost foot by
foot, and an intelligent scheme conceived in all its ramifications, before anything is done.

The course of a path may be determined by so many considerations that we should be certain none have been overlooked before committing ourselves to any apparently advantageous plan. The path from the entrance gate to the house should never connect with another path, so as to leave a stranger in doubt which route to follow when entering or leaving the premises. When it is necessary for some reason to connect another path with that leading from the gate to the house, any ambiguity of purpose can generally be avoided by making the connection at right angles, as by this arrangement it is evident that the destinations of the two paths are separate and that the main objects, the house and the gate, can not in common-sense be connected by a path that turns a square corner, instead of that which continues its easy curve. However, there is another means of avoiding connections that are misleading: by making the less important path much the narrower of the two, though we would advise the employment of both expedients, especially if the subordinate path leads to some necessary but unattractive spot, such as the back door, the kitchen garden, or the wood-shed. Of course, in such a case as that illustrated in Fig. 7, where the grounds are so small that the visitor can not go astray, these precautions are unnecessary, though even in this instance we would, as indicated, make the path to the back entrance narrower, and so plant our shrubbery as to conceal its destination. Much more might be said about the general planning and relative treatment of paths, but we have, perhaps, occupied the reader long enough in this discussion without describing the methods of making and maintaining good roads and paths.

A good driveway or path is one that is so made as to always retain its slightly convex form, and to be dry at all times, even immediately after a heavy rain—so made that, even where steep grades exist, the heaviest rain can not wash away or furrow the surface, leaving a miniature torrent bed to be filled and civilized. The drive or path must be first excavated in its whole width, nowhere less than one foot deep, and in the center not less than two feet deep, forming a trench with shelving sides. This trench must be graded in depth for the whole length, so as to become a channel in which water will run off. In paths of any length on a level, it is usually best to grade in two directions from a central point, while on a slope the trench can be of the same depth throughout. This trench should be filled with stone to within six inches of the finished surface, as indicated in the annexed cut, Fig. 8, the large stones being selected and placed at the bottom, so as to form an unobstructed drain, and the stones should decrease in size upward until the interstices are filled with large pebbles screened from coarse gravel; the whole surface should have a slightly convex form, as shown in Fig. 8, and the work is complete when three or four inches of clean gravel have been well packed by heavy rolling, and an inch or two of finer screened gravel have been added in the same way. It is of the first importance that the

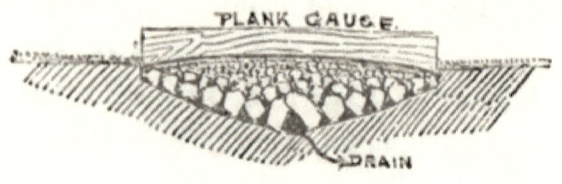

FIG. 8.

gravel used should be clean, that is, free from loam which will cake when wet and form mud, while no water can possibly remain on the surface of a drive or path constructed as we have described.

The most convenient way of determining the convexity of the surface and of maintaining uniformity throughout, is to have a "gauge," made of a plank exactly the length of the width of the path ; one edge of this plank is cut to the desired curve, which, when applied at any point, will show deviations. The simplest method of laying out paths on the ground is to set out a row of stakes or pegs on the center line in the whole length and at sufficiently short distances, say five feet, apart to enable the curves of the path to be seen at a glance. The positions of the pegs can be altered until a satisfactory sweep or any desired tortuous line is attained, when the edge of the path on each side can be established by similar rows of pegs, whose exact position can be determined by the ends of a stick or pole of the requisite length, the the length being the width of the path. A notch or mark of some kind is made in the center of the stick, which, when applied to the central row of pegs at right angles with the direction of the path must describe at its ends the same curve as the center line. Fig. 9 indicates

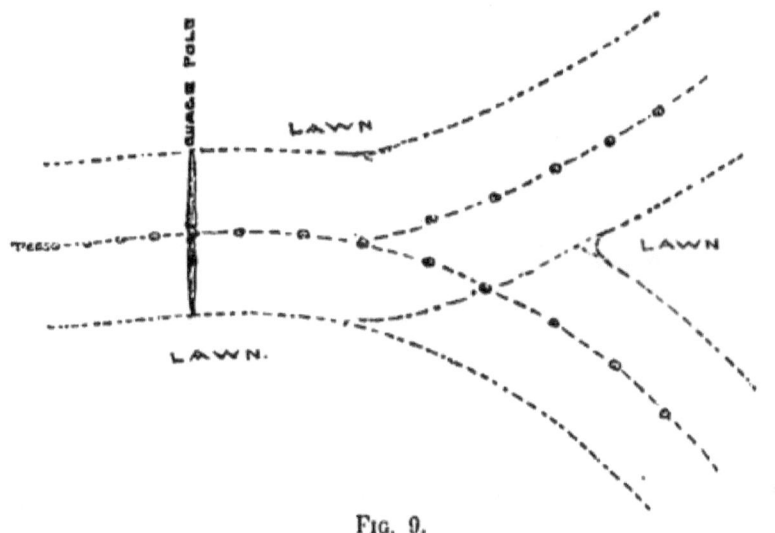

Fig. 9.

this process, which, in grounds of small extent, is a simple and rapid one. Where much woodland or objects of any kind obstruct the view so that we can not see the curve for more than a short distance, it is necessary by measurement and calculation to establish the center line as we have drawn it on paper; but the general reader would probably pass over geometric formulæ, so that we shall content ourselves with a simple explanation of how to lay out a circular curve when, for any reason, we can not drive a stake in the ground, attach one end of a rope, and run round with the other. If the relative positions and distances of the points at which our circular curve begins and ends can be set down upon paper to some appreciable scale, as shown in Fig. 10 at A and B, we can easily determine what portion of the circumfer-

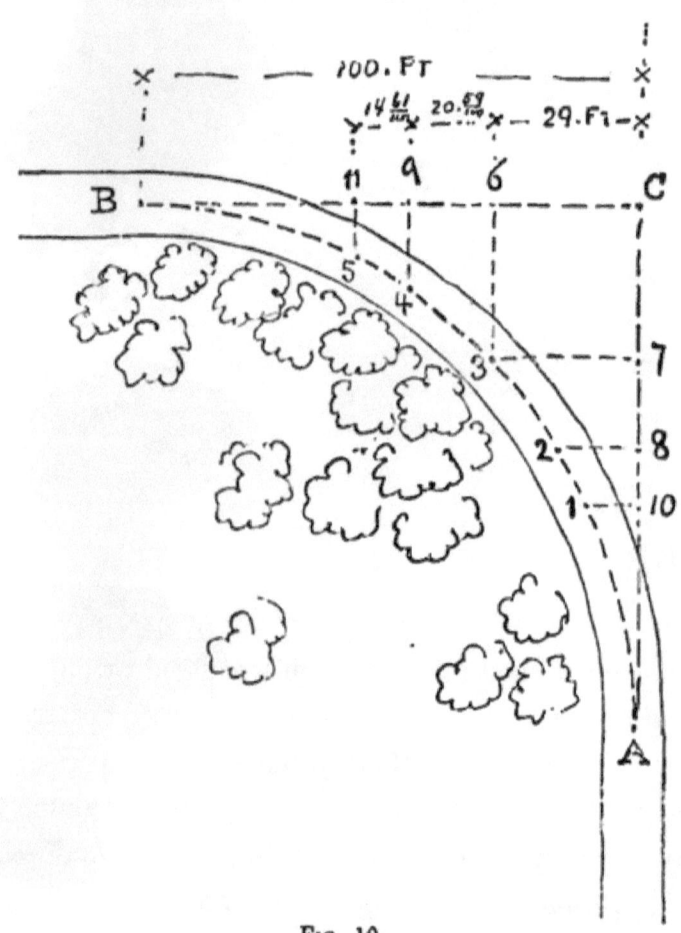

Fig. 10.

ence of a circle our curve shall be in order to die into the straight lines at these points, and also to circumvent the trees or other objects whose existence makes the change

of direction necessary. Fig. 10 represents the plan of a
road around woodland or rocks where it is necessary to
change the direction from A to B at right angles, without
disturbing the objects that intercept the view, and in
order to achieve a proper curve both A and B are continued till they meet at C, that is, their central rows of pegs
are continued to this point. The distances from C to 6
and C to 7 are then measured off toward A and B, and
are always, whatever the actual distance, in the proportion of 0·29 : 1. For instance, suppose the distance from
A to C to be one hundred feet, then the distance from C
to 6 or to 7 will be twenty-nine feet ; from these points,
6 and 7, parallel to AC and AB, the same distance is set
off, and establishes the point 3 in the center of the curve.
In the same way the points 1, 2, 4, and 5 are determined,
and as many intermediate ones as are desired. When a
double curve or S is necessary, the same process is repeated in the opposite direction, only that the point 3
must be determined as the center of the S, as indicated
in Fig. 11.

The importance of true curves in laying out roads or
paths is not a mere question of effect, but one of practical
convenience, because in driving, walking, or riding we
shall find that in changing the direction of our route we
necessarily describe a curve, and not an abrupt one. In
fact, at any considerable speed, it is difficult to describe
any but a generous circular curve of, say, fifty to one
hundred and fifty feet radius, and anything less than fifty

feet may be considered as too abrupt for a driveway, though, of course, in paths there are many considerations making almost any form desirable under peculiar circumstances.

In making paths on a rapid slope or hillside, it will generally be found cheaper and more picturesque to introduce three or more broad stone steps at intervals, rather

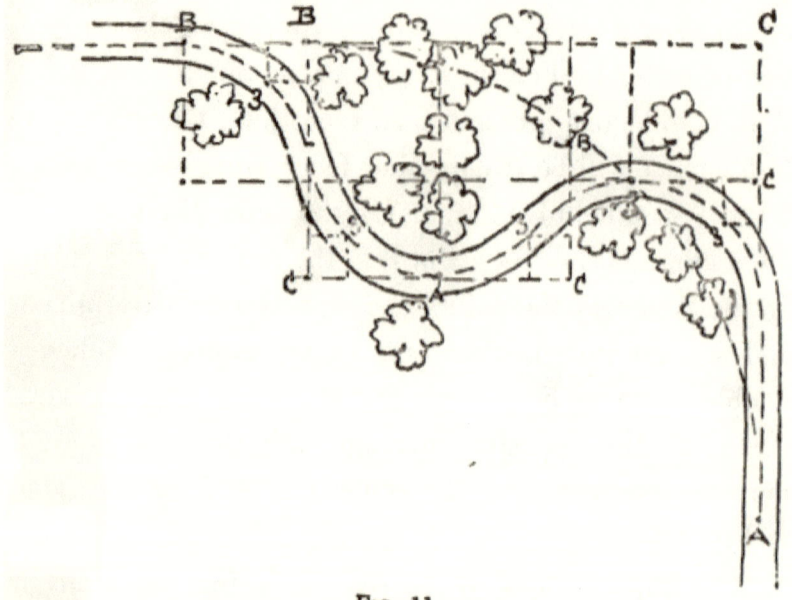

Fig. 11.

than to attempt an even grade throughout, and much more convenient than to follow the variations of the surface. By introducing the steps, the walk in the intervals can be kept almost level, while the differences of level between the several parts and the adjoining ground afford many valuable opportunities for effective planting, and

4

the whole walk, viewed from either end or from other
parts of the grounds, becomes an object of much greater
interest than a mere strip of gravel, however graceful in
plan, could possibly be. This arrangement is a step in
the direction of the formal château garden, with its terraces and staircases, but, if only employed in situations
that make it practicably desirable, it has none of the artificial ostentation of the elaborate *parterre*.

III

LAWNS AND GRASS PLOTS.

In the foregoing we have so constantly alluded to the importance of well-kept turf as an element of successful landscape gardening, and have incidentally discussed so many effects more or less dependent upon the form and extent of lawns and grass plots, that little more than instructions for preparing and maintaining good turf under various conditions remains to be stated.

The paradoxical adage that the shortest road is the longest way round finds corroboration in the various methods of making lawns, of which the most generally practiced is that of cutting slabs of the best turf the neighboring waysides afford, preparing the ground, packing them down and watering them from time to time until the transplantation has taken root. This method is no doubt an expeditious one, but has few other advantages. We know of but one satisfactory way to produce a healthy and hardy turf, and but one of maintaining it. The process is comparatively a long one, though not more expensive than the almost universal method described above. There are few soils in which a

good turf can not be made to grow in time if the necessary care is bestowed, and a soil in which we can not
grow turf without enrichments will certainly fail to support transplanted turf. Whatever the nature of the soil,
it should first be plowed and stones removed, then har-
rowed and sown with "red top." This should be done
as early in the year as the season permits, and the crop
should be allowed to grow till the seed is nearly ripe,
when the whole, as it stands, should be plowed into the
land, the harrowing repeated, and the best grass seed
thickly sown, mixed with small white clover seed. This
crop again should be allowed to run almost to seed before
it is cut. The cutting should be done while the dew is
still on the grass, and the crop should lie where it falls,
to be withered by the sun. This cutting or mowing may
then be repeated at intervals of ten days or a fortnight,
but *no raking should ever be done.* The hay performs
the most valuable services. The turf grows through it
so that in one season a complete net-work of hay covers
the ground beneath the fresh young grass and protects
the roots from the sun. The advantages are obvious;
the turf is denser and much less sensitive to drought,
as the hay holds a good deal of moisture after every
rain, which rots it into manure; this, together with our
protecting net-work of hay, is constantly replaced by the
periodical mowing. After two years of the above processes, we can do nothing better for our lawns than to
suspend the mowing for a season and substitute the nib-

bling of a sufficient number of Southdown sheep to insure impartial grazing over the whole area. The constant
pattering of so many harmless feet will do more satisfactory work than any amount of rolling, while the drop-
pings become a thoroughly distributed manure. Thus it
will be seen that under ordinary conditions a perfect and
permanent lawn can be made in three years, after which
time the usual mowing at intervals of two to three
weeks, according to the weather, must be kept up and
performed in the manner at first described, viz., before
the dew is dried and without removing the cut grass.
The sheep dose may be advantageously repeated at intervals of two or three years, or for a short time during
every season. There are some sources of annoyance in
new lawns that can only be cured by constant and watch-
ful care during the second, third, and fourth years. We
refer to the appearance and spread of dandelion and
plantain, both of which are familiar to every one, and
are not without special medicinal value, though they mar
the beauty of a lawn. Whenever one of these weeds
shows itself, it should be cut out with a knife to the depth
of three or four inches, and a piece of rock-salt inserted,
which will prevent the reappearance for a considerable
area about that spot. For a time yellow patches will appear when the salt has been used, but these will soon pass
away, and, if the obnoxious weeds are diligently hunted
down in this way, their race, as far as our lawns are con-
cerned, can be exterminated for ever after two or three

campaigns. This weed difficulty is one of the objections
to transplanted turf, which, however prepossessing in appearance, may, like adopted children, develop the most
trying and distressing tendencies for all the care and
education spent upon them. While, if we can not sit
in the shade on our lawn, as we have described it, after
training it up in the way it should grow, we shall at
least have more pleasure for our pains than we could
realize in any other part of our improvements with the
same outlay, to say nothing of the fact that all other improvements would tell for nothing without our velvet
turf.

A lawn is capable of so many effects that it may be
useful to attempt some classification and some analysis of
them, so that the causes may be recognized, and to some
extent manufactured at pleasure. Of course there are no
effects that can not be enhanced or modified by judicious
planting and by other means, but we propose first to discuss such effects as are wholly due to the lawn itself,
resulting from its form in plan, the character of its surface, whether level, graded, or undulating, and its innumerable gradations of color, all of which qualities it
will be seen are more or less co-dependent, so that, in
appreciating any effect, each of these qualities must be
considered in its relative importance. We have already
said, in the discussion of driveways and paths, that the
forms of our lawns and grass plots result from the lines
adopted for the paths, which lines should be determined

by the effects produced in our lawns as much as by the numerous considerations involved in the uses and objects of paths. Fortunately, and we may say naturally, the desirable forms for lawns are best arrived at by serving the uses and objects of paths, that is, the sweeps and curves we have advised for the laying out of paths are the most effective boundary lines for lawns. In cases where a lack of simplicity is felt owing to an unusual number of curves in the lines of paths, and where these curves can not well be dispensed with, we may restore the needed repose to our lawns by judicious planting; a strong straight line of close hedgerow, as formal as trimmed arbor-vitæ, is often a pleasing terminus to a strip of lawn which might otherwise have a sprawling or crawling expression as of some great prostrated animal; and, again, where a bend in a path seems to take a notch out of the otherwise flowing outline of our lawn, an interesting copse of well-selected foliage can be interposed. In general, any regular form for a lawn is unfortunate in effect; the question of its actual extent, as with the entire grounds, should be left undetermined. Of all forms, the square, or in short any parallelogram, should be avoided. For small grass plots in close proximity to the house, the circle and all elliptical forms are often useful, especially in the management of driveways, but few forms are more pleasing in perspective and more easily managed than the varieties of the pear shape. Fig. 5 shows an arrangement of lawns and paths mainly composed of this

latter form, which affords more effective opportunities for
planting than any other, while it results from the easiest
and most effective lines of communication for paths and
drives.

The great artistic value of the lawn is its ever-varying
tones of color, first, in the mere gradations of foreground
and middle distance, then in the gradations resulting
from undulations of surface, and lastly from the strong
effects of contrast resulting from the shadows of the
planting. Of these last effects we shall have more to say
when discussing planting, but the gradations of color on
an undulating surface and on a level offer the landscape
gardener inexhaustible opportunities for displaying his
skill. Nature is his model as she is the painter's, but
she is also his ally, and will glaze his picture for him
with all her qualities of sunlight from dawn to dark. If
his actual distances are too short for the effects he aims
at, he must model his ground so that the shade side of
his knolls and undulations at all times of day may pre-
serve the values necessary to the perspective he has manufactured. This manufacturing perspective is a much
simpler thing than would generally be supposed. We
know that the predominance of yellow in a perspective
composition is a quality of foreground, and blue that of
distance, which is only another way of saying that yellow
is the strongest quality of light; therefore when the sun
shines upon an undulating surface of grass, we shall see
the shadows or shade sides in blue-greens, while the

lights or sunlit sides will appear as yellow-greens. These facts enable us to so model our lawn as to lend distance to the farthest points and prominence to the nearest, always assuming the positions from which the effect will most constantly be seen.

If a lawn is large enough, say at least an acre in itself, the beautiful gradations of a dead level are appreciable, but in smaller spaces it is difficult to get rid of a sense of formality and flatness, though, of course, almost any defect of this kind can be much mitigated, if not altogether obviated, by planting, as the shadows can prevent the monotony of a mere green carpet of apparently one hue throughout.

The practice of breaking up lawn surfaces with flower beds is, to say the least, very ineffective. We see many places whose simplicity and real beauty are marred by uneasy patches in the center of almost every available grass plot. We will not undertake to lay down invariable rules for these dispositions, but, in general, the less ornamentation employed in landscape gardening, the better the effect will be. There are shrubs and plants that are occasionally very effective in emphasizing a particular spot, or by contrast lending the desired effect to other foliage, which at a greater or less distance acts as its background; but nothing can be gained by parti-colored patches here and there, looking like pieces of worsted work, and entirely destroying the effect of *ensemble* by their strong assertion; and it must be remembered that, even if the spots of color furnished by these flower beds were desirable in our scheme, they can only be counted on for their short season, and consequently our effect at other times is incomplete.

When flowering plants are used on the lawn or grass plot, it is much better that they should apparently grow directly from the turf, or be placed in pots, tubs, or vases of such character and material as shall assist instead of defacing our surface, as the spots of earth in flower beds must inevitably do. Nature knows better; she shows us her flowers in banks of moss, on grassy slopes, on crags of rock, or mirrored in a pool, and, though we may choose to have a flower garden to supply us with cut flowers and growing plants in our *jardinières*, we can not do better in our landscape gardening than to follow her example in this as in all effects. We may, of course, aim at the achievement of a scheme that shall have its spring, its summer, its autumn, and even its winter aspect, all of which shall be attractive; in fact, no scheme of garden improvement can be considered successful that has not the faculty of wearing its various garbs becomingly. Nor is such an achievement the most difficult part of our task; we shall find that it is as easy to select the colors and all the details for our several seasons, if only we have planned and modeled well, as it is to select effective costumes for a well-proportioned, graceful woman. All our general effects of plan and disposition, if satisfactory during one season, will, as in nature, certainly remain so during the next. It is only in the selection of trees, shrubs, plants, and vines that we can exercise the discretion and fore-sight when once we are committed to our scheme of arrangement. .

Some of the most successful grounds we have seen are laid out in the simplest fashion—a single broad drive-way from the gate to the house and thence to the stable being the only gravel surface, the rest of the place being devoted to a broad expanse of perfectly kept turf, upon which groves, copses, hedges, and here and there a broad-spreading oak or a pair of arching elms are distributed or clustered, so as to provide various effects, from the densest shade to the breeziest common, and vistas so managed that there is always a sunlit glade beyond.

IV

PLANTING.

" Where to the eye three well-marked distances
    Spread their peculiar coloring—vivid green,
    Warm brown, and black opaque, the foreground bears
    Conspicuous; sober olive coldly marks
    The second distance; thence the third declines
    In softer blue, or, lessening still, is lost
    In fainted purple.   When thy taste is called
    To deck a scene where Nature's self presents
    All these distinct gradations, then rejoice
    As does the painter, and, like him, apply
    Thy colors; plant thou on each separate part
    Its proper foliage."

THE art of disposing our trees and shrubs so that
they shall not only display their own beauties to advantage by the relative position of different varieties, but
shall emphasize the best points of the plan adopted, and
carry out the most effective dispositions, is the crowning
work of the landscape gardener.   Before selecting from
the varieties available, he must determine the general
form of each copse, thicket, hedge, or tree, must have a
clear conception of the effects he desires, both as a whole

and in detail. In the several illustrations already referred to, dotted lines are shown radiating from the important points of view, such as the porch of the house, the bay-windows, and from some points of the entrance path, or drive. In following these lines it will be noticed that they explain the effective reasons for the dispositions of the planting, and suggest the vistas that have been arranged on these sight lines. In planting, as in all else, one must begin at the bottom and work upward; the first things to be determined are the individual and relative position of each tree or clump, then the respective form of each in plan—that is, how much ground they shall cover, and in what form. The next question is the shape of the growth, or its silhouette against the sky. Then the character of the foliage, as a whole, and in detail, and, lastly, how far we shall compose so as to bring out particular shrubs or trees against the rest of our planting, as a background.

The general effects to be avoided in planting are dispositions that subdivide our lawn in any regular way—in other words, symmetry, or any disposition that suggests a system of spacing, robs the landscape of the natural element. We often see in mountainous country the most charming effects of lawns, woodlands, and shrubbery on distant hillsides, sufficiently distant to soften and smooth the rough and unkempt effects that undoubtedly exist on the spot. It is such effects as these that we can realize in our gardens, and add to them many interesting

and beautiful details. Much of our planting may not be
a matter of choice, but of necessity where there are
neighboring objects which it is desirable to screen, and in
such cases we must make up for any loss of freedom of
effect by an artistic arrangement of the thicket or hedge.
A beautiful view of distant hills may often be much enhanced by the foreground we oppose, our varieties of
trees, shrubs, and vines enabling us to design and realize
almost any outline for our foreground and middle-dis-
tance foliage, as well as to determine their relations of
color. Fig. 12 and Fig. 13 are illustrations of what we

Fig. 12.

have said in regard to form and character of foliage.
For color we would refer the reader to nature, and we

trust that what we have said, and what we are about to say, in describing the principal varieties of trees, shrubs, and vines, may make the realization of natural beauties somewhat easier. It must be remembered that both

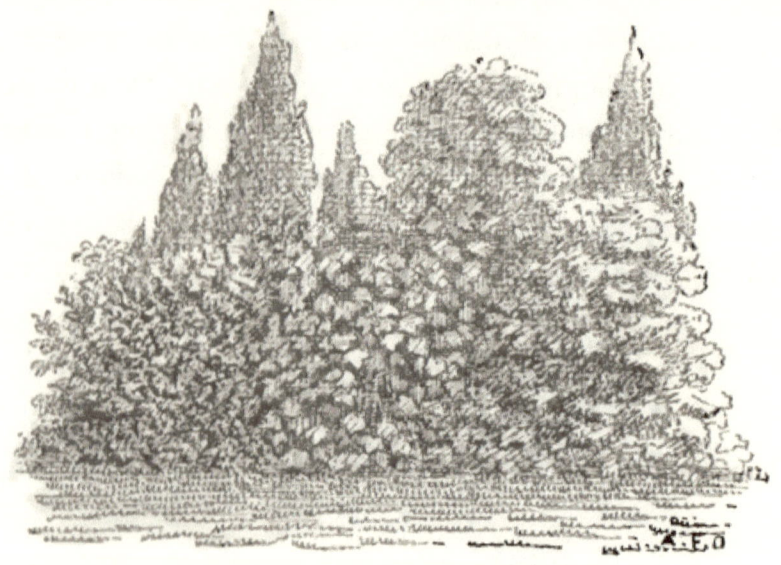

Fig. 13.

form and color can be made valuable without. foliage— that many of the most beautiful landscape effects are to be seen in winter when the evergreen is the only surviving green. The character and color of bark are also important elements of effect in summer as well as in winter, if the trees are in positions to display their trunks, or if they rise above other vegetation so as to expose their larger branches. The gardener is fortunate who is assisted in his improvements by a few existing fine old trees, and, when he lays out what remains for him to do,

he should think twice before hiding behind shrubbery
the gnarled and mellow effects that it has taken so many
years to accomplish, and which will make such a pleasing
contrast rising out of a rich, fresh turf. In any scheme
of improvement, however limited the extent of the
grounds, it is more effective to conceal the house from
the entrance gate as a standpoint, and from some other
points of the entrance path on its approach, so that the
visitor may catch glimpses of the building here and
there through the planting before he reaches a point at
which the whole is apparent. There are other advantages in such dispositions than those of effect—private
advantages to the occupants of the house, especially in
small places, for, when the gate latch is heard to rise and
fall, the visitor may be recognized as he passes the openings in the shrubbery, and may be admitted or denied
admission accordingly. Any one can escape from the
porch or veranda in time without subjecting the visitor
to the annoyance of seeing his host or hostess fly at his
approach. In some places of large extent, where the
sound of the gate is not audible as far as the house, a bell
is arranged, which the visitor unconsciously rings by
opening the gate, and this idea could now be enlarged
upon to include a telephone so as to save unnecessary
steps.

The illustration of entrance gates that we have used as
the frontispiece to this book is a portrait of the entrance
to Fig. 5, and is published by the special permission of the

author's former partner, Mr. Bassett Jones, and, although
the gateway itself is rather more imposing and expensive
than is usual or than would be appropriate for small
grounds, the general effect of the planting is a good
example of the treatment we would advise to conceal the
house, and give the effect of dense vegetation on entering the premises. Of course, the large trees in this
instance have accomplished more than half the work, but
even where these do not exist, and can not be acquired
for many years, the desired result can be approximated to
with such hardy, rapid-growing young trees and shrubs
as can be procured and transplanted. In regard to the
outline of any tree or shrub, or of a clump, what can not
be accomplished by selecting the right varieties for the
form we desire must be done with the pruning-knife,
and often by the employment of vines growing on the
trees. Almost all trees and shrubs grow according to
the space surrounding them. If confined on all sides,
they shoot upward for light and air, and assume entirely
different forms and proportions from those they would
acquire in an open space; so, if confined on three sides,
the growth will be toward the fourth, especially if that is
the sunny side.

This faculty of vegetation of taking any general form
we may desire, in its instinctive reaching for light and
air, enables us to produce a great variety of effects with
a small variety of plants, and this is the more fortunate because it is difficult, expensive, and often practi-

cally impossible to make certain things grow in every situation; so that, even where our means are unlimited, we shall often meet with disappointments in transplanting. It is usually safer to note the indigenous varieties, and largely adhere to them. There are localities in which many kinds of familiar common trees, for reasons more or less incomprehensible, do not thrive, and other situations in which only a limited variety can live at all. Some limitations of this kind can be obviated by changing the nature of the soil, either by mixing in the necessary enrichments to a sufficient depth, or by raising the level of the whole ground with the necessary quantity of earth of the right sort; but these are improvements that involve expense. In exposed situations, such as the seashore, river-banks, and hill-tops—in short, in all situations exposed to the keener winter storms—the hardiest vegetation should, as far as possible, be so disposed as to shield the half-hardy and more sensitive on the north and east. Large trees, dense shrubbery, and hedgerows can also be made to act as bulwarks for the house in the same way, and whichever is first established—the house or the trees—should, to a great extent, determine the position of the other, at all events, if the house is occupied in winter, which may be the case with any house, whether it is built solely as a summer-house or not.

It has not yet become common to plant a garden with any special view to the various seasons, and we would suggest the idea of a spring garden in which the branches

shall be still without foliage, though of all hues, from the
many grays and browns of the old bark to the innumerable tints of browns, greens, and reds of the twigs—occasionally contrasted with the white bark of the silver
birch, with its dark and graceful branches. With all this,
and against the net-work of twigs and switches as a background, should stand out the white blossoms of the dogwood, the pink flowers of the Daphne, the flowering
almond, and all shrubs and trees that blossom early before they leaf. Such an effect would be tiresome if per-
petual, but for its short season could be more beautiful
than any other. Then, as the early summer comes, these
first blossoms will fall; but, while they are fast disappear-
ing, the apple-trees, peach-trees, and cherry-trees bloom
out, and, with the horse-chestnuts, make another display
of color softened by the fresh greens of the new leaves,
and so we pass on through all the deepening tones of summer till the first frost sets our thickets all ablaze with
gold and scarlet, making the effects during the winter
season seem hushed and cold. When the snow lies un-
broken over the whole landscape, and suggests, in its
rounded, glistening way, all that it so softly covers, we
shall find effects at sunset of each short day, in looking
through the bare boughs at the western sky, that may not
enliven us as much as our spring picture, but they en-
lighten us much more.

TREES, ETC.

WE would not be understood to mean, by anything we have said in the previous chapter, that we advise the coaxing and forcing of trees into forms that are unnatural for them to assume, but the contrary; and we believe that any desired form of vegetation can be grown if the trees, shrubs, and vines are selected with due regard to their peculiarities, and are cared for with an appreciation of their requirements. There is a vast difference between letting a place run wild, and, by judicious pruning and propping, enabling each variety of tree and shrub to attain its healthiest development. Our descriptive lists of trees, shrubs, and vines available for landscape gardening in the United States do not pretend to be exhaustive, but merely to mention the material for planting that can usually be found at the nurseries, while the descriptions are intended to enable any one to recognize what he may desire to select without previous study. The lists are arranged alphabetically for convenient reference under four heads, viz.: "Trees" (deciduous), "Evergreens," "Shrubs," and "Vines." Any directions for the cultivation of flowers or description of varieties is beyond the compass of this small volume, and would require to be discussed in a more technical manner than we have assumed in these pages. We may, however, say, for the benefit of those who are especially interested in horticulture, without having any scientific knowledge to assist them, that flowers thrive best in sand well manured, exposed to the morning sun, and sheltered by vegetation or buildings from the northern and northeastern storms. Under these conditions, if the weeds are uprooted, the surface disturbed daily, water supplied early in the morning and at sundown, and the flowers cut with a sharp knife as soon as they are developed, there can be little difficulty in having a plentiful supply, always providing that the roots have plenty of room. Overcrowding in the garden or too small pots will not be attended with blooming results. In regard to fruit-trees, fruit-bearing bushes, vines, and plants, we shall discuss them only from the decorative point of view, as fruit growing can hardly be considered as a branch of landscape gardening.

DESCRIPTIVE LIST OF TREES (DECIDUOUS).

AILANTUS.—This tree is sufficiently familiar in almost all parts of the United States to require little description. We have already mentioned some of its objectionable peculiarities, to which may be added a more or less offensive odor. It is, however, not without virtues, being particularly clean and exempt from the attacks of insects or worms, and is one of the most rapid growers for the first ten years. As a full-grown tree it assumes a graceful form, and its peculiar fern-like foliage is often very effective.

Apple-trees are not particularly valuable as features in landscape gardening till they have attained an old age, when the tortuous forms assumed by many varieties are extremely picturesque. An old apple-tree in full blossom is a beautiful feature on a lawn, and later in the season, when its branches are laden with brilliant red or golden fruit, contrasting with its clustering dark-green leaves, it becomes a very ornamental object.

Ash.—Of this tree there are many varieties, of which the most beautiful are the white ash with its abundant bluish-green foliage and picturesque trunk, its small branches and small leaves turning purple in the autumn; the weeping ash, with drooping branches, abundant, dark, glossy foliage and irregular, straggling growth; the golden ash, so called from the color its foliage assumes with the first autumn frost, in other respects much resembling the white ash, except that it does not attain so great size and has larger branches. The Mountain ash is also very decorative, with large clusters of white blossoms in May and scarlet berries in autumn.

Aspen.—This tree is properly a variety of poplar, and is described under that head hereafter, as also the "Balm of Gilead."

Bass.—This is one of the most valuable trees to the

landscape gardener, having a beautiful, clean trunk, a graceful, rounded form, and large, glossy, heart-shaped leaves. This tree is also called the "linden," and another variety in which the leaves are of a brighter green and much glossier is called the "grape-leaved linden," because the leaves are more varied in form.

BEECH.—There are several varieties of the beech-tree found in America, the most interesting of which for gardening are the weeping beech, the "purple-leaved beech," and the "fern-leaved beech." The trunk of the beech-tree is particularly effective in landscape, with its gray, mottled bark, so smooth and clean. The weeping beech is irregular, pendent, and luxurious in growth, its foliage, like the "purple-leaved beech," being glossy. The foliage of all beech-trees is small, dark, and smooth, though always brilliant, and turns to a rich umber.

BIRCH.—The most useful of the birches in landscape work is the canoe or paper birch, with which every one is familiar. Its slender, graceful, silver trunk and dark red-brown branches, together with its small, dark, but silver-lined leaves, often afford a gleaming effect in a thicket of other and larger foliage that is extremely effective. Its tendency, already mentioned, of sending up shoots in all directions makes it as troublesome on a lawn as it is valuable in a thicket.

BLACK-WALNUT.—This tree is unmanageable in landscape work, owing to its selfish propensity in destroying almost all other surrounding vegetation, including grass.

This is the more to be regretted, because the tree is a handsome one and attains great size.

The same objection can be made in a lesser degree to the butternut-tree, which, however, is not so handsome as the black-walnut, its foliage resembling the varieties of ash to the unbotanical eye. Both these trees have sufficient commercial value and beauty of texture and color in their wood to atone for their unavailable peculiarities in landscape gardening.

CATALPA.—This tree is a native of the South, and, though not fully hardy, is a valuable lawn tree. It grows very rapidly, spreading to a beautiful rounded form, with trunk and limbs of a delicate brown; its beautiful clusters of violet blossoms, and its large, velvety, heart-shaped, pale-green leaves make a most decorative effect. In exposed situations it is necessary to stay and prop the branches to prevent their being broken in wind storms, but these contrivances are hidden by the luxuriant foliage, which affords an ample shade, and survives the most scorching sun that withers almost all other vegetation.

CHESTNUT.—This tree is as valuable as the oak for landscape-gardening purposes; its fine massy foliage and its greenish-yellow blossoms make it very ornamental. When young, its stem is smooth and its foliage clear and bright, and in old age it attains majestic size. The Spanish chestnut is a small tree, rarely attaining in this country a greater height than forty feet, and then only in a mild climate; it is, however, a luxuriant and beautiful tree, often available where the ordinary chestnut would not be so effective.

CHERRY.—The varieties of cherry-trees are more marked in their fruit than in their general appearance, and, while every one appreciates the preference for the cultivated fruit, the wild-cherry is much the most picturesque tree, at least while young; its leaves and branches are darker and glossier, and it grows in a more graceful form.

COFFEE-TREE—so named because the first Kentucky pioneers used the seeds as a substitute for coffee—is a very beautiful tree, bearing white blossoms early in summer, and having doubly compound leaves three feet long, of a bluish-green. It takes a finely rounded form, and grows to about sixty feet in height in northern latitudes.

CYPRESS.—This tree is very common in the Southern States, and does not thrive farther north than New York City; it is, however, a very interesting and beautiful tree for landscape work, being conical in youth and always luxuriant, its foliage being of a light, rich green. There is a specimen in the Bertram Garden, in Philadelphia, one hundred and thirty feet high and twenty-five feet in circumference. Its peculiar rugged trunk, with conical excrescences, makes it a picturesque addition to any collection, and a grove of cypress is very impressive.

DOGWOOD.—This tree, though a small one, is one of the most decorative—its curious, picturesque forms and its large blossoms are familiar in all parts of America—

and is often seen in full blossom in a mass of evergreens, whose society it seems to find congenial in contradistinction to most other trees.

Elm.—The elm is of all American trees the most graceful, especially the weeping or white elm, which abounds in the Berkshire hills in Massachusetts, and has been so often mentioned by the poets and story-tellers. There are, however, many other varieties, all of which can be successfully grown in America. The red or slippery elm is a small and not a luxuriant tree, and is not valuable for landscape work; but the wahoo elm, though small, is a rapid grower and a picturesque tree. The English elm is also a beautiful tree, and spreads finely, and for some effects the small compact and upright "purple-leaved elm" is very useful. There are also the Scotch weeping elm, much like our own and many other varieties, which are curiosities like the "twisted elm" and the "gold- and silver-striped elms," with variegated leaves.

Ginko, or Salisburia.—This is originally a Chinese variety, but has been successfully grown in America as far north as Boston, for nearly a century. The foliage is very like the maiden-hair fern, only much larger, of a pale yellow green; the general form is conical, and it attains great size.

Horse-Chestnut.—Of this beautiful tree there are many varieties, differing in size, in hardiness, and in the color and profusion of blossoms, but they are all decorative, though we have not as yet in this country produced specimens to compare with the finest in Europe. The varieties are: the Ohio buckeye, small size, yellow flowers with red stamens; the "red-flowered" is small, with scarlet flowers; the "smooth-leaved" has pale yellow flowers. The "red- and yellow-flowered Pavia" of the South are pretty varieties, but the common tree, with its bunches of white blossoms, is the finest of all. The horse-chestnut is so called because in Turkey the nuts are ground into meal for broken-winded horses, and it was from Turkey in Asia that the tree was first introduced into England, where there are now the finest specimens in the world. The Avenue in Hyde Park, when the horse-chestnuts are in bloom, is a sight worth crossing the water for. The trees stand free, rising out of a rich turf to a great height like a procession of verdant flowering bee-hives as the branches droop almost to the ground, while, with the sun on the decline, their foliage and their deep shadow make a wonderful gradation of color.

HICKORY.—The most ornamental species are the shell-bark hickory, the pig-nut and the pecan-nut; all of these assume beautiful forms, and grow to large trees. The bark of the shell-bark hickory is very peculiar, becoming almost detached from the trunk in large scales. The nuts of this tree, which are universally familiar, used to be called the Kisky-tom nut by the old Dutch settlers. The pecan-nut hickory has the largest leaves, often

eighteen inches long, of a brilliant green. All the hick-
ories, but the Southern water bitter-nut, have beautiful
large foliage, and are effective garden trees.

Locust.—Besides the exceeding value of its wood, the
locust is a very beautiful tree, putting out white fragrant
blossoms in June, and delicate pinnated bluish-green
leaves. There are various opinions as to its ornamental
pretensions, but we notice that nature always shows us a
clump of locusts which is certainly beautiful.

Larch.—This is a resinous, cone-bearing tree of the
pine family, but, unlike them, sheds its leaves, which
grow in bunches and are a bright, light green, while the
branches and twigs are a rich red brown. It is a rapid
grower, and a very picturesque pyramidal lawn tree.

Lime.—This is another name for the linden or bass-
wood tree, already described. There are five or six varieties of these trees, all large-leaved and beautiful; the
Susquehanna River, Pennsylvania, variety, with its silvery bark, is, perhaps, the finest for garden embellish-
ment.

Three-thorned Locust, or Acacia.—This tree has
many advantages as a lawn tree over the ordinary locust,
though it has not the same beautiful blossoms, but its
foliage is more luxuriant, and it assumes a variety of
picturesque forms, sometimes a pyramid of sixty feet,
and again a low horizontally-branched tree. It does not
produce suckers like the locust, which makes it less
troublesome.

JUDAS.—This tree grows only about twenty feet high, and is covered with pink blossoms early in the spring, before the leaves have expanded; from this fact it is often popularly called "red bud." There are two varieties, the American and the European; the latter has darker and less pointed leaves.

MAPLE.—Maples are rapid growers, and have not only luxuriant, brilliant foliage, but a variety of beautiful trunks. The trees are sure to assume good forms if allowed sufficient room, and not the least of their merits as garden trees consist in their autumnal tints and the clustering growth of the leaves. There are in America no less than nine varieties, of which, perhaps, the scarlet maple is the finest, though the white maple is more umbrageous. The silver-leafed maple is beautiful in the same way that the silver poplar is valuable, while we could find a great deal to say upon the subject of the sugar maple, which, even when robbed of its plentiful sap, still finds means to become a fine tree, frequently turning half yellow and half red, unlike other kinds, in autumn. It is not, however, a proper lawn tree in comparison with those we have mentioned, though its trunk in maturity is handsomer.

MAGNOLIA.—This is one of the most beautiful and various of all vegetation; there are many varieties, from those with leaves only a few inches in length to those whose leaves are even two feet long. The variety of forms, both of flowers and leaves, seems unlimited, as well as the colors of the blossoms; some have a delicious perfume. In the South magnolia-trees reach an altitude of seventy feet, and a blossoming grove is a beautiful sight. Some varieties are evergreens.

MULBERRY (Paper).—This is the only variety of mulberry that is valuable as a garden tree. Its peculiar interest consists in the different forms assumed by the leaves, no two being exactly alike. It looks like an exotic, as it really is, being indigenous to Japan and the South Sea Islands. It grows rapidly to about thirty feet, and bears red berries.

OAK.—To attain its greatest development and beauty, the oak requires ample space, free exposure to sun and air, and deep, rich soil. Evelyn in his "Sylva" says: "The incomparable uses of this wood were needless to enumerate; but so. precious was the esteem of it of old, there was an express law among the twelve tables concerning the very gathering of the acorns, though they should be fallen on another man's ground. The land and the sea do sufficiently speak for the improvement of this excellent material, for houses and ships, cities and navies are builded with it." There are no less than forty varieties in America; the "live oak," "Spanish oak," "red oak," and "white oak" are the finest.

OSAGE ORANGE.—A very beautiful Southern tree, sometimes attaining sixty feet in height; the branches are light-colored, with spines at every joint. The leaves are long, ovate, and pointed, of a deep green, and glossier than the orange. Its branches are wide-spreading and far apart, so that it is not dense.

PEPPERIDGE, TUPELO, or SOUR-GUM TREE, is one of the varieties of gum-trees, and recommends itself to the landscape gardener for its glossy, dark-green foliage, and the brilliant flame color it takes on with autumn. The black-gum tree has larger leaves, and is a larger tree, but can not live in the North.

PERSIMMON.—This is a useful addition to the garden, with its dark-green, glossy leaves some five inches long; it is somewhat like an orange-tree in appearance, though larger, often attaining fifty feet in height.

PAULOWNIA.—This tree is a native of Japan, and is remarkable for the great size of its heart-shaped leaves and its rapid growth. It produces panicled clusters of bluish lilac blossoms in abundance and of pleasant odor.

PEAR.—The varieties of pear-trees are too numerous to be here set down, especially as artistically there are none of them valuable in gardening. They often assume picturesque forms in old age, but their place can be supplied.

PEACH.—The artistic value of the peach-tree is mainly in its blossoms, and for their sake it may well be included in our spring effects.

PLANE, or BUTTON-WOOD.—This is a broad, umbrageous tree of great size. It has a habit of shedding its bark in patches, suggesting Bryant's lines:

" Clear are the depths where its eddies play,
And dimples deepen and whirl away,
And the plane-tree's speckled arms o'ershoot
The swifter current that mines its root."

POPLAR.—Poplars are rapid growers and small leaved,
but present a great variety of forms. The Lombardy
poplar, as Proctor says, "Shoots up its spire, and shakes
its leaves in the sun." The aspen also has this peculi-
arity. The silver poplar is, on the contrary, a broad, umbrageous tree with a silvery bark, and leaves silvered on
the under side, making a glistening effect in a bright,
breezy day. There are twelve other varieties, including
the "Balm of Gilead," with its large, heart-shaped leaves.

SASSAFRAS.—This tree is much like the European
laurel or sweet-bay. Its blossoms, which appear in May,
are yellow, in small clusters; the leaves are oval or three-
lobed, of a deep, glossy green, and, though it is a comparatively small tree of rather irregular form, it is very
decorative and well suited to the garden.

SWEET-GUM.—This tree is not unlike the maple in
appearance. During the whole summer its dense foliage retains a dark glossy freshness, and in autumn turns
to a deep purplish-red, darker or lighter, and occasionally
to a brilliant orange. This difference in its autumnal
tints makes it especially valuable with other trees, as it
supplies at this season tones to be had in no other foliage.

SYCAMORE.—This is a large tree, large-leaved, and

light in color, both as to leaves and bark, the latter being provided with a sort of grayish-brown covering that peels off in patches, leaving a chalk-white exposed, and giving the tree an ill-used look; in form the tree is good, but on the whole ineffective.

THORN-TREE.—This is frequently little more than a shrub, but, like the hawthorn, if given room will grow to thirty feet. The foliage is glossy and dark and very various in form, growing in tufts, and, in the early season, snowy blossoms appear in profusion. The fruit is deep-crimson or purple, and very decorative.

TULIP, or WHITE WOOD.—This tree is properly of the magnolia family, though larger than they. Its foliage is rich and glossy, and is peculiar in form, each leaf being six to eight inches in width, with two-sided lobes. The blossoms are like large tulips, borne singly on the young shoots, and are very brilliant.

VIRGILIA.—This tree is of the locust description, with pinnated leaves; the foliage is dense, and the height attained is about forty feet. It is more beautiful than most of the trees with pinnated leaves, and has a profusion of white blossoms.

WALNUT (European) is much like our black-walnut in appearance, and is no less a large, fast-growing tree; its foliage is dense, and of a russet hue in May, turning later to a yellow-green, so that it is one of the useful trees for many effects, though it loses its leaves very early.

WILLOW.—This is a comprehensive word applied to

many varieties, from a small shrub to large trees.   Of
these latter, there are a dozen kinds or more available,
but the color and character of the foliage make it difficult to use them effectively in a garden, especially a small
one.

EVERGREENS.

Arbor-Vitæ.—The American variety of this tree
(often called the white cedar) is naturally of a beautiful pyramidal form, branching close to the ground.   Its
thick, flat, and abundant foliage of a rich green is only
slightly browned by severe frost, and in summer submits
to the shears better than almost any other tree or shrub.
For hedges and often for copse planting, the arbor-vitæ
is invaluable; as a single tree in open ground it is less
effective.

Cedar.—The red cedar is the best known and most
useful variety, assuming a great number of different
forms, according to the soil and situation, from a broad-
spreading, picturesque tree to a conical and formal one.
The foliage assumes many colors at different seasons and
on different trees, as a lively green, a deep-green, a blue-
green, and a brown; its density and richness are distinct
from the same qualities in the arbor-vitæ, and are equally
valuable in landscape work.

Fir.—Firs are divided into two classes—the spruce
firs and the silver firs.   The difference between pines
and firs is that the leaves of the firs are shorter and
are attached all round the twigs, the whole tree being

more conical in form. Of the spruce firs there are many varieties, of which, perhaps, the finest American natives are the "black" and "red." The Norway spruce fir is the most frequently planted for ornamental purposes, and is certainly as handsome an evergreen as can be, and among the grandest of trees in maturity. The spruce firs also include the hemlocks, which are of many forms and peculiarities, round-headed, conical, and straggling, but always graceful or picturesque and hardy, to say nothing of their agreeable fragrance, in which they resemble the balsam silver fir. For landscape purposes the silver firs, except some dwarf varieties, as shrubs, are not valuable.

HOLLY.—This name is common to species of all sizes, from shrubs to trees, mostly evergreens. The characteristics of the European Christmas holly are sufficiently familiar, but it is not hardy, and can not be employed, as it is in England, in hedge-rows, trees, and bushes, north of Maryland. The American holly is very similar, but still a Southern native.

PINE.—Of this large family there are as many as fifty varieties, including the natives of all countries, and many subdivisions could be made under varying circumstances. Of American pines, the white pine is undoubtedly the grandest and most beautiful of all, and secondly the yellow pine of our Southern States, whose brilliant foliage and vigorous growth result, especially when a number of trees are planted *en masse*, in an effect of exotic pic-

turesqueness. Pines are distinguished from other evergreens by a longer leaf or needle, and in these needles
growing in bunches of three, five, or more from a sort of
sheath. Occasionally the less important varieties have
great value for certain effects. Even the scrub-pine,
that grows in a stunted and grotesque manner on the
sea-shore, is interesting on a lawn from its very straggling appearance. On Long Island specimens can be
seen that grow upward for some four or five feet and
return to the ground, where they take a tortuous, snake-
like form for several yards before shooting, or rather
bending, upward again.

YEW.—Of the yew family there are some twenty
members, none, however, in this country attaining anything like the proportions of the English yews; but
among them are found many ornamental, small evergreens that are useful to prevent monotony. The foliage is like the fir family, but the leaves are longer and
thicker, the whole mass being denser and richer.

EVERGREEN BERBERRY.—This is a particularly ornamental tree or shrub, has dark-green, shining foliage,
and deep-orange flowers in the spring. There are others
that do not present these peculiarities, as, for instance,
the sweet-fruited berberry, which is more a shrub, but
still an ornamental variety.

JUNIPER.—This tree is properly, in all its variations,
a member of the cedar family, but is peculiar in its compact, vertical growth and acute, conical form. The most

decorative variety is the Irish juniper, which, however, requires protection both from extreme exposure to sun and to frost. It is well fitted to mark the angle formed by two paths in open ground, but not for close planting.

SHRUBS.

Althea.—This shrub recommends itself, if for no other reason than that it blooms in August and September, when others are stripped of blossoms. It is a broad-headed, rather stiff than graceful shrub, but among the eight or more varieties there are several very decorative.

Amorpha.—This is a very showy half-hardy shrub, with spikes of purple and violet blossoms sprinkled with yellow, appearing, according to the variety, from June to August. There are some seven varieties, of which one, "canescens," bears blue flowers in July and August. The leaves are small, like locust leaves, in pairs of leaflets.

Andromedas.—This shrub is also a deciduous tree and also an evergreen, both tree and shrub. Of the deciduous shrub the most desirable varieties are the "L. racemosa," with its white fragrant flowers in June and July, and the "L. Mariana," with pink-tinged flowers from May to August.

Aralia.—This is very decorative on account of its large leaves and luxuriant growth. It has been called the angelica-tree and also the Hercules club, the latter name from its annual canes that resemble thorny clubs.

7

Arbutus.—This is an evergreen with drooping red blossoms as late as December, and scarlet fruit. In England this shrub becomes a tree thirty feet high, and our "A. procera" variety attains twenty feet.

Azalea.—This is one of the earliest blossoming shrubs, and one of the most beautiful. There are more than twenty varieties bearing as many different colored blossoms.

Boxwood.—Who ever has seen an old colonial garden must remember the little hedges bordering all the walks, but these are not the natural shrubs, but what the shears have made them. The small, glossy evergreen leaves, the dense growth, and the accommodating character of boxwood, make it one of the most useful of shrubs.

Daphne.—In March, before any leaves appear, the daphne decks itself in brilliant red blossoms. There is a variety that blooms in November and December, and has larger leaves than the earlier shrub. The only objection to the daphne is that its leaves and berries are poisonous.

Deutzia.—This is a small flowering shrub, originally from Japan, and somewhat like the syringa. It flowers in June, either white or pink, and some varieties attain twelve feet in height.

Dwarf Almond.—This is a small shrub, blooming before it leafs in March, when the dark-brown twigs are covered with rose-pink blossoms. The leaves are like peach leaves, though smaller, and the shrub has no value as an ornament before or after it blooms.

HONEYSUCKLE.—This is one of the *sine quibus non* for all gardens, with its abundant beautiful foliage, its sweet blossoms, and its early habit. There are many varieties, but none finer than the "red Tartarian."

JASMINE.—

> " The deep dark green of whose unvarnished leaf
>   Makes more conspicuous, and illumes the more,
>   The bright profusion of her scattered stars."—*Cowper.*

There are trees, shrubs, and vines of this name, all more or less beautiful, and with fragrant blossoms, some varieties only emitting fragrance at night. Of the shrubs there are those that bloom from May to October, and those that bloom from June to August.

LILAC.—This familiar shrub is as indispensable as the honeysuckle. Among the common and the Persian lilacs we find the leaves larger or smaller, lighter or darker, glossy or velvet, and the habit bushy or upright, but all bear beautiful blossoms, ranging in color from white through all shades of lavender and violet to a deep red purple. The "rothmagensis" is considered the finest specimen.

LAUREL.—The pink and white flowering mountain laurel, which grows in abundance in Berkshire, has been successfully transplanted, and is a valuable addition to ornamental vegetation when not in bloom ; its rich, glossy foliage is beautiful.

KALMIA.—This is another name for the above, which

is found not only in Berkshire and similar situations in the North, but is common in the Gulf States.

Quince.—This little tree is regarded as a fruit-bearer, but its claims to being classed as a rich ornament will always be admitted when in full blossom, or when its large golden fruit is ripe.

Rose.—Of this numerous family we would only say that some members can be considered and treated as shrubs with charming effect, especially if massed in quantity and well selected for hardiness and color.

Spiræa.—This common wild shrub has justly become a favorite for its many colors, both of leaves and flowers, according to the variety selected. The family is large; its members often bear little resemblance to each other, but among them are many very beautiful flowering shrubs.

Staphylia.—As a rapid grower and spreading bush the staphylia is very useful; its flowers are small and white, but its leaves are of good color and decoratively arranged in a mass that is often twelve feet in height.

Syringa.—We may class this fragrant shrub with the honeysuckle, as a matter of course, in every garden; and certainly a garden like Mr. Longfellow's, with nothing but a mass of lilacs, honeysuckle, and syringa among the old elm-trees, is attractive enough without rare specimens.

Rhododendron.—This family is perhaps the richest of flowering shrubs; its thick, glossy, large leaves are a fine setting for its clustered flowers, ranging in color from white to pink, yellow, lilac, crimson, and deep purple. The blooming months are May to August.

VIBURNUM.—This is what is commonly called the snow-ball, from its round masses of white June flowers. The shrub is showy and of good form, but we are inclined to think it unimportant.

WEIGELA.—Of this Japanese shrub we have already many varieties, and they have many qualities to recommend them. The flowers appear in June, and are either white, pink, or red. The growth is rapid and bushy, attaining a breadth and height of ten feet.

In the foregoing we have only attempted to suggest a few names that may be useful in carrying out such effects as we have described from time to time. For anything like a complete list of shrubs alone would require more pages than we have devoted to our whole discussion, and those who require more precise and copious information must turn from our pages to more scientific works, but in our lists will be found sufficient material to produce almost any desired result, while they will serve as a basis for more extended study. We shall presently give the titles of a few works that we can recommend to those who desire to go deeper in all or any of the questions that are touched upon in these pages, as this small work is necessarily little more than an introduction to a number of scientific studies.

VINES.

BIRTHWORT.—This vine is invaluable for covering trestle-work in summer-houses and for attaining massive effects of foliage; it twines and climbs to great heights, bears a profusion of large heart-shaped leaves, and in May and June blossoms of a yellow-brown color shaped like a hook.

BITTER-SWEET.—This is a strong climber, capable of killing young trees; bears glossy, pointed leaves, and in June violet blossoms. It is, however, most showy in autumn, when the berries are numerous, of a deep orange color.

CLEMATIS.—There are a dozen or more varieties of this vine, bearing larger or smaller leaves, and blossoms having more or less fragrance and size. They are all delicate and beautiful vines.

EVERGREEN IVY.—This beautiful vine has been so often celebrated by the poets and is so familiar as to require little description. It does not survive hot, dry summers nor very cold winters, but can be protected by northern exposure in summer and by straw in winter, though it never attains its luxuriant English growth in America.

GRAPE.—The grape-vine has been used to cover, or rather imperfectly conceal, so many hideous painted structures that its beauties have not been fully recognized in America. The Clinton and the Concord vines are the hardiest and most serviceable varieties for decorative purposes.

Hop.—The ordinary hop-vine is one of the most serviceable of decorative vines, on account of its rapid growth and the facility of planting from cuttings or seed. The leaves are much like miniature grape leaves—abundant and of a bright light-green. During its short life of four or five months it will climb to a height of forty feet.

Trumpet.—This familiar creeper is mainly valuable for its large trumpet-shaped orange flowers that appear in August and September. It has the same faculty as the Virginia Creeper of adhering to the bark of trees and walls.

Virginia Creeper.—This is at once one of the most luxuriant and most beautiful of all vines, growing rapidly to the height of seventy or eighty feet in less than ten years, where a tree or tower affords a foothold for its innumerable tendrils and roots.

Woodbine.—The woodbine is properly of the honeysuckle family, of which there are many fragrant and beautiful varieties. The flowers of the woodbine are most showy, being deep red outside and buff inside.

Wistaria.—Of this beautiful vine there are many varieties with blue or violet flowers appearing in the commonest sorts from July to September. The Chinese Wistaria grows more rapidly than almost any other vine, and is thoroughly hardy. Most astonishing stories are told of old vines in China with trunks seven feet in circumference, while the growth extends over immense areas of trellis and buildings. We have seen instances in this country that inferentially corroborate these statements, when it is remembered that our oldest vines can not boast more than forty years.

CREEPING or PROSTRATE JUNIPER.—This is very useful in covering rocks with a deep, soft carpet. It is an evergreen and a rapid grower, presenting various shades of warm green in different seasons, but requires shade for perfect development.

TRAILING ARBUTUS.—This is a very beautiful wild creeper, growing under conditions that are not easily provided on small grounds (moist, deep soil, with accumulations of dead leaves), but it would be worth much trouble to add this beautiful pink-flowering, sweet-scented vine to the early spring attractions of our grounds.

The foregoing lists have been inserted merely to suggest what a judicious choice of trees, shrubs, and vines can accomplish, even in very small grounds, at all seasons. We have only thought it necessary in such an elementary book as this to name a small number of the innumerable varieties, but we have intended to select such as can usually be provided, and such as are the most effective. A comparison of the peculiarities and habits of the trees, shrubs, and vines that we have named will suggest the idea that it is quite possible to plant a garden that shall assume a peculiar and attractive appearance during each season. In this art of landscape gardening nature will provide many delightful surprises for the inexperienced if only a fair chance for development is given in establishing favorable conditions, and without more scientific information than we have given in our early chapters these conditions can easily be realized.

VI

FENCES AND GATES.

THE various ways of enclosing grounds are as numerous as the various conditions that make some sort of fence or barrier desirable, and consequently no particular description of barrier can be recommended as the best in all cases.

The conditions that require the establishment of a fence, a wall, a hedge, or ditch, with or without an earthwork or parapet, are of two kinds, viz. : conditions resulting from arrangements within the grounds, and those resulting externally. These two kinds can, of course, be subdivided into practical and artistic conditions which are *not* always easily reconciled.

In well-ordered populous communities no barriers are required to protect the gardens from the inroads of straying cattle, while in many summer retreats this is an important consideration that must be substantially met with stout rails or stone walls.

Where a real and effective barrier is necessary for the above or for other reasons, a dry stone wall (built without mortar) is at once the most durable and the most

practical solution of the problem, and no objection can
be made to it on the ground of artistic effect, as, if well
built of such stones as the region affords, it is in itself a
picturesque object, and can be beautifully clad with blossoming vines, making a pleasing termination to the lawn
within, and an interesting wayside spectacle without.
The expense of building a wall in regular masonry, with
proper cut copings, foundations, etc., generally precludes
such undertakings, and, except in cases of rare occurrence,
no advantage is gained by them, either practically or artistically; on the contrary, the most thorough masonry,
exposed on both sides as in a boundary wall, will require
repairs from time to time to prevent the inevitable
effects of frost from disintegrating the construction; so
that it is not only much more costly than a dry wall, but
is a constant source of annoyance and expense, while
it does not afford so good a hold for vines as the dry
wall, and many vines, such, for instance, as the ivy and
the woodbine, will in time eat out the mortar joints.
Where public highways or adjoining property is on a
lower level than the enclosed garden, and where the
nature of the ground or other conditions make a natural
slope or sodded embankment impracticable, a breast or
retaining wall is unavoidable, but even in such cases a
dry wall is, for many of the reasons already stated,
preferable to a wall of masonry. The object of a breast
wall is to retain the earth in position, and the force ex-
erted against it tends to push it outward, so that the best

form to adopt is that shown in the annexed cut, Fig. 14, in which the beds of the courses of stone are shown to

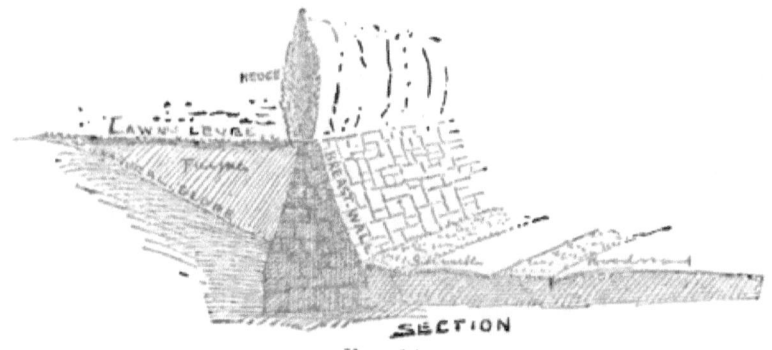

Fig. 14.

incline inward, so as to add some of the weight of the stones to the resistance of the wall, on top of which, and on the level of the grounds, a fence, hedge, or additional wall can be set up if desired.

Of fences the choice lies between wood and iron of various modes of construction in detail, the principle of equidistant posts or supports secured in the ground being common to all fences of whatever material. The best fence is that which best serves its purpose at the least cost, and consequently the palm must be given to the rustic fence, which is as durable as any other, not more expensive at the outset, and does not require painting from time to time, as all other fences do, while it is of an agreeable color, and readily lends itself to the scheme of a good design. The proper height for a fence is a question to be determined by the peculiarities of each

case. For the ordinary purpose of a barrier, four feet
six is high enough, but, if a screen is required, less than
seven feet is of little service; of course the higher the
fence the more frequent must be the posts, and the
deeper they must be sunk, so that additional height is
more than proportionally expensive.

As to the design of a fence, the first requisites are
strength and durability; nothing can add to the beauty

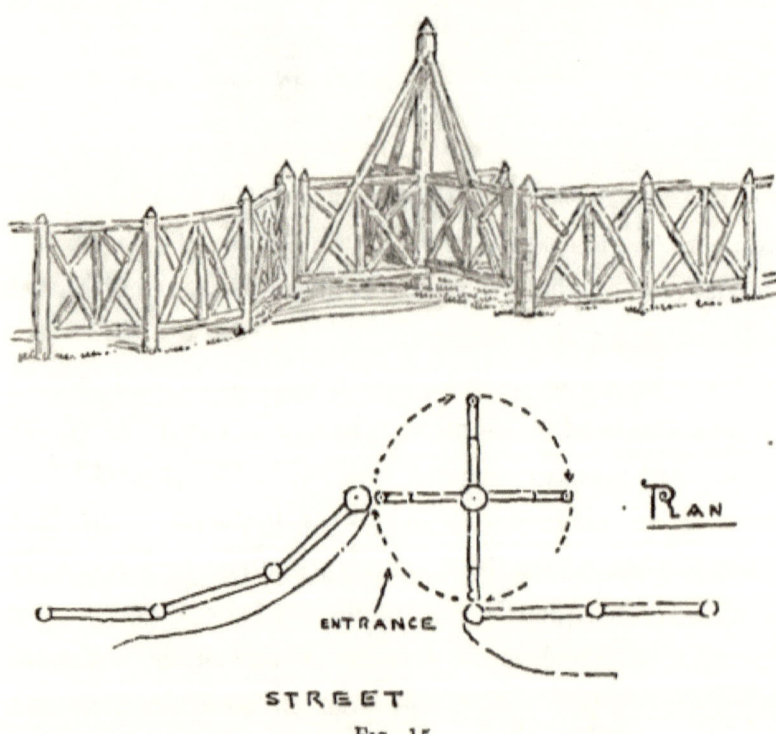

Fig. 15.

of a design that does not serve some definite purpose;
the various systems of bracing a frame afford ample opportunity for effective treatment without adding useless

members with the delusive intention of ornamenting the
construction, which should, and can easily, be in itself
ornamental. Figs. 15, 16, and 17 are suggestions for

Fig. 16.

fences that may serve to show how innumerable are the
forms that can be arranged in bracing and tying the top
and bottom rails that must exist in all fences.

If for some reason the rustic fence is undesirable, and
a more or less elaborate piece of carpenter work is to be
indulged in, few better treatments can be devised than
is suggested in Fig. 18, a more or less faithful portrait of
an old colonial fence still standing near Portsmouth, N.
H.—still standing because the builders were wise enough
to use nothing but locust wood in the construction ; and,
though locust is among the more expensive woods, it
pays best in the end, and requires no paint, which can
never give the fine color and beautiful texture that the
wood assumes when exposed.

Of iron fences the lightest wire description is often useful between two gardens, as it is almost invisible and enables neighbors to reciprocally lend larger effects than either could realize if the dividing line is determined by a conspicuous barrier. Even the iron fence is, in many

FIG. 17.

localities, entirely dispensed with, a community of gardens being formed within certain limits. In this way all participants enjoy a real park at much lighter cost individually than they could keep up the appearance of small gardens. By comparatively small contributions to a common fund a competent corps of gardeners can be employed, and, if the paths, roadways, and planting are cleverly managed, the views from the most important points on each property embrace what appears to be an extended pleasure ground, without a suggestion of mere shareholding. Of course it may be objected that this is an ostentatious advantage, and that a man should not desire to appear to live beyond his means, but there is

another view of the matter; from the nature of the case
there is and can be no deception as to the facts, and it is

certainly better for the several owners, for their visitors,
and for the passer-by, that there should exist a single and
effective scheme of improvement in which the houses
are so situated and designed as to form additional points
of interest in a picturesque sense, rather than that, for
the small and unimportant purpose of gauging each
owner's limited domain, and inferentially his means, there
should exist a number of contiguous pens more or less
successfully subdivided and adorned.

The sense of landlordism is one that is so dear to
some people that no benefit to themselves or others could
pursuade them to dispense with clearly-defined boundaries
to any land they may be possessed of; and, even in localities where land is not worth a hundred dollars an acre,
men can be found who will spend years of their lives
and many times the value of their property in litiga-

tion over the setting of a fence one foot farther north or south.

Where fences are a necessity, there is seldom a good reason for uniformity of design in the fences on all sides; on the contrary, the conditions existing toward different points of the compass would naturally suggest as many styles of fencing, hedges, or walls, as there are boundary lines; in fact, the greatest variety in this respect is often desirable, both practically and artistically, even to building a wall twenty feet high on one side, while on another no stronger limitation than a trimly-kept walk may exist. Many beautiful things may adorn the adjoining acres which we would like to avail ourselves of in perspective, if it were not that they are accompanied by other things more or less disgusting. This is often the case with large trees, in whose shade hovels and pig-pens have accumulated. In such cases a high wall, vine-clad within, at once shuts out the revolting spectacle below, and adds a certain mysterious interest to the trees above, especially if we provide a postern-door in our wall, which can be made a very suggestive feature, especially to those who are jealous of privacy. In this particular Americans are peculiar, in comparison with Englishmen. The latter is never happier than in owning a square mile, with his house in the middle; and, when his property is bounded by the highway, he prefers to have a barrier so high that no passer can form any opinion of what exists within. Americans, on the contrary, concern themselves rather

too much with outward appearances, and are as anxious
that their places should look attractive from the public
highway as they are of being able to see from their veran-
das or porches all that transpires beyond their domains.
This question of indifference or sensitiveness to the public gaze is one for each man to decide for himself, but we
can at least expect that whatever is set up as a screen
shall not be a hideous barren spot on the roadside. When
a man can afford, for selfish reasons, to build a high wall
on the roadside, he can at least make as much concession
to public taste as to build something not more uninteresting on the outside than the wall suggested in Fig.
19, in which there is economy of material as compared
with an unbroken dead surface, the piers really doing the
work while the intermediate curtains perform the office
of screens. This idea can be developed to almost any extent, so that the spaces or panels between the piers may
be made to accommodate seats, and, by an over-hanging
coping or roof, these become shelters that are philan-
thropic institutions outside and picturesque garden features within. Such an arrangement is suggested in Fig. 20,
and though, as shown, it would be a costly wall to build,
much of the same general effect can be realized in simpler ways; such, for instance, as building a low wall, and
carrying up a close trellis-work above in wood, and covering thickly with such vines as woodbine, Virginia creeper,
bitter-sweet, etc.—in short, such as will soon form a close
network of twigs and tendrils that fill the apertures of

the trellis even in winter, and become dense and luxuriant in summer. Among the most practically effective
screens and barriers is a close hedge-row of arbor-vitæ,
with a complete system of large wires concealed in the
foliage, and stretched in their whole length from occa-
sional iron bars or rods set in flat stones and also concealed
in the hedge. Upon this hedge all manner of vines may
be allowed to grow, and while both sides are picturesque,
the screen is as complete as any wall could be—to say
nothing of the advantages in economy at the outset, and
the absence of all repairs.

The gateway being the point of interest in any fence,
is necessarily the controlling idea in designing the fence,
and we should have discussed gates before enlarging
upon fences, were it not that gates are much more difficult things to treat successfully, and much that we have
said of fences simplifies and elucidates what we would
say of gates. From the simple turnstile to such elaborate and costly undertakings as the one depicted in our
frontispiece, there is sufficient scope to meet every possible condition, and any complete discussion of the subject,
illustrating the innumerable ingenious and beautiful ex-
amples that exist, would fill a larger volume than this, so
that we must content ourselves with describing a few designs, and explaining the principles that they illustrate.
In Figs. 15, 16, 17, 18, and 20, five different gates are
shown, adapted to the peculiarities of each case, but
in reality the gates are in every instance, except Fig. 20,

the key-note, and the fences are designed in accordance. It is comparatively easy to design a good fence, because

Fig. 19.

its first principle is immobility, while a gate must not only be strong and durable, but must readily perform its office of opening and shutting. Every one is familiar with the old country methods of a chain and ball whose weight closes the gate, and also of the older method of dispensing with hinges, and prolonging the top rail to receive a weight of stone, so that the gate balances on one post, and, when once lifted, can be swung round on a pivot. The practical objections to these primitive methods are several, but mainly that they both demand the exercise of more or less physical force, and in the case of the ball and chain the necessity of holding the gate open until one is fairly beyond the reach of its jaws, in going out to avoid being caught, and on entering to avoid being fairly kicked into the garden. Another objection to the ball and chain is that the gate is necessarily made to swing outward, and one is obliged to unlatch the gate and then move backward until the opening is

Fig. 20.

large enough to enter; the same difficulty would be experienced in going out, if the gate swings the other way, so that it is necessary to have it hung to swing in both directions. The usual solution of this problem is to hang the gate on a single pivot at top and on a double bearing below, so that the point of rest or gravity is only attained when the gate is shut. One of the objections to this method is the facility of unshipping the gate, which constitutes a standing temptation to mischievous boys; another is the annoyance of hearing the prolonged gyrations backward and forward whenever any one passes through.

As most people are as unlikely to shut a gate as a door after them, some automatic provision is desirable, and we believe that nothing more satisfactory can well be devised than an adaptation of the old-fashioned turnstile for foot-passenger gates, while for carriage entrances we have yet to see any really satisfactory automatic arrangement. The adaptation of the turnstile is shown in Fig. 15, and in Fig. 16 the canopy above admits of the simple expedient of lines and pullies, the weight on the lines being just sufficient to counterbalance the gate, and insure a slow return to its closed position. This is an adaptation of the old ball-and-chain idea without some of its disadvantages, and can easily be applied to large carriage-gates. If it were not for accumulations of ice and snow in winter, the automatic-rod arrangement would be more satisfactory than any other. This consists of a rod connection with the roadway some twenty feet distant on each side of the entrance, so that the wheel of the approaching vehicle passes over an elbow, and causes a quarter revolution of the crank at the gate-post, the reverse action on the other side closing the gate when the carriage has passed through and runs over the other elbow. For places only occupied in summer this is entirely satisfactory, but in winter it requires as much care to keep the action in working order as to open the gate by hand. A litch-gate, such as is shown in Fig. 16, can be well arranged to hang from above, and run on a track and wheels like a barn-door, and this offers opportunities for picturesque treatment, as the whole construction is pendent, and the usual reasons for tieing and bracing are changed from cross strains into tensile strains.

For entrances to chicken yards and such other enclosures, where the convenience of visitors is not to be considered, the old-fashioned stile has many advantages in being to all but human animals as effective a barrier as the fence or wall itself. It is hardly necessary to add, after all that has been said, that it is seldom advisable to fence off any portion of a garden from the rest, unless in the cases of a kitchen garden or a chicken run, and for this purpose a dense hedge is at once more serviceable and more attractive, with such openings as may be necessarily cut through, and filled with a rustic gate. For such hedges the arbor-vitæ, already mentioned, is as satisfactory as any growth, but, if it has been used elsewhere on the boundaries of the place, it is better to have a variety of effect by using such shrubs as the Newcastle and Washington thorns, the buckthorn, the Osage orange, or the privet. Of course, there is no limit to the variety of beautiful effects that can be attained by mingling various shrubs in one hedge, and growing vines of all sorts over the whole mass of foliage. In planting a hedge-row there is seldom any necessity for adhering to an un-broken straight line in plan on both sides, and many rich effects of light and shade can be realized by adopting a varied line, tortuous and angular, making the hedge pre-sent the appearance of a few rich clumps of shrubbery connected by hedge-rows. To many people a clipped formal hedge, as nearly as possible like a green wall, is particularly handsome, and we do not say that it has not many advantages under certain conditions; but, in gen-eral, we do not believe in substituting geometric or other artificial forms for the natural graces of vegetation. This artificial treatment is distinctly different from judi-cious pruning and training, to prevent trees, shrubs, and vines from developing some unhappy tendency that would defeat the efforts we make to achieve certain picturesque results well within the bounds of natural de-velopment.

VII

SUMMER-HOUSES, SHELTERS, ETC.

THE uses of summer-houses and of shelters are at least four: 1st, to protect one from the sun while sitting out of doors without hat or umbrella; 2d, to enable one to enjoy whatever breeze may be stirring from any quarter, not felt on the veranda owing to the position of the house; 3d, to mark the most advantageous points of view that the gardens or the surrounding country can be seen from; and, 4th, to embellish the grounds with forms and colors unattainable in planting. Therefore, the design and the position of these structures are not to be arbitrarily determined, but are a part of the scheme of improvement, and are suggested by its conditions. In very small gardens it is questionable whether it is ever desirable to erect any artificial structure besides the house, because an extremely small summer-house is very nearly useless, and a large one dwarfs the premises. It is better in such cases to design the gateway as a shelter, and provide seats on each side; in this way importance is given to the entrance, and the shelter encumbers the garden as little as possible; of course, in many localities the public

9

street is too much frequented, and becomes too dusty to
make such an arrangement agreeable, but where these
objections do not exist it is the best compromise we
know of. We have seen all manner of fancies indulged
in summer-houses, from the rudest rustic shelter to the
most elaborate models of the Tower of the Winds or
the choragic monument of Lysicrates executed in marble,
and while grottoes and miniature temples have a certain
place in the artificial garden about a *rénaissance* palace
or *château*, they are utterly incongruous in such undertakings as this volume treats of.

Where a natural formation presents a picturesque opportunity, we would in almost all cases take advantage
of it, and even enhance its effect by any means at command, but we would under no circumstances attempt to
manufacture a freak of nature. In designing summer-
houses, nothing is gained by attempting to make the
structure look as if it grew as we have fashioned it;
first, because such attempts are futile, and, second, because one of the beauties of a good design of this sort
is its ingenious, thoughtful construction in the midst of
natural forms.

Good summer-houses can be built by any country
carpenter out of any saplings that may be at hand, but
the best and most durable are built of cedar with the
bark left on. Occasionally a few trees, notably apple-
trees, may be found in such relative positions that it is
possible to make them the main lines of a summer-house,

and without injuring the trees. Observatories can often
be well managed in old trees, especially such as are dead
at the top, their bald heads offering many forks in which
to rest the logs for the staging or floor of the look-out.

WIGWAM SHELTER
Fig. 21.

Wells and springs may very properly be made an ex-
cuse for rustic structures, and the opportunities for em-
bellishment become inexhaustible with the assistance of
blossoming vines; though it should always be remem-

bered that, however decorative and fragrant vines may be, they harbor insects of all sorts, including mosquitoes, so that generally a place to sit in, either a summer-house or a veranda, is more comfortable without them. Any spot that is exposed to a fair breeze can not be infested with mosquitoes, as these pests are very weak on the wing, and can only indulge their sanguinary tastes in sheltered places or on motionless days.

Of the countless summer-houses in existence, some of the best specimens are to be found in the New York

Fig. 22.

Central Park and in the Brooklyn Prospect Park. By the kind permission of Mr. Vaux we are enabled to give an illustration of the sort of thing we refer to, Fig. 24, in which by very simple means a very happy result has been achieved. The structures illustrated in Figs. 21, 22, and 23 require no special comment, being all rough sketches of shelters erected by the author at various places. In Fig. 23, the upper portion is designed for a bird-house, and is now inhabited by a large and quarrelsome family of sparrows, who, to a great extent, have obviated the nuisance of insects among the vines that

Fig. 23.

climb the screen on one side toward the southwest, so that a shady nook is provided for the summer afternoons, commanding an extended view of a Berkshire valley on

the southeast.   The upper portion of Fig. 21 could easily
be used, with a few additional sticks, for a bird-house,
without altering its wigwam character; on the contrary,

Design for a Rustic She'ter.—C. Vaux, Architect.

Fig. 24.

such addition would improve it, and mitigate its extremely primitive and rudimentary expression.

Where a seat is desirable without a shelter or summer-house, we do not think that the picturesque effect of rustic work in so small a matter compensates for the almost inevitable discomfort of the seat, and we would advise the employment of more carefully devised carpenter-work, resulting in more comfort, and not necessarily in less artistic effect. There can be no objection, in such small objects as settees or chairs, to employing well-selected colors, and painting them in rich reds or warm sienna tones; in fact, some such spot of color is often as much needed in a landscape as in a picture, only let us, like the painter, try to put it in the right place, and as nearly as possible of the right tone. This matter of tone or balance of color enters in some form into all arts, and while there are some favored few whom nature has endowed with delicate senses, and who have trained their perception till it has become an unerring instinct, most people are in this respect a good deal like the two boys of whom their mother said, "John! he don't know nothing, but Henry, he does"; so that it is difficult to say which knew the most.

The whole matter of seats, shelters, summer-houses, and trellis-work can so easily be overdone, giving a place a crowded and uneasy effect, that we are inclined to advise their use only when their absence is a manifest inconvenience or artistic omission.

VIII

CHICKENS AND CHICKEN-HOUSES.

For all that may be said of the nuisance of crowing cocks, it is always our neighbor's cock that disturbs our morning's doze, and there is an undeniable luxury in breakfast-eggs that are above suspicion, which the city denizen rarely enjoys. Many householders in the suburbs and in the country would devote some portion of their gardens and their time to the maintenance and care of chickens, if there were apparently any reliable proportion between the number of chickens and the supply of eggs; but where chickens are not properly cared for, and allowed to range about, they become cackling, crowing, and unprofitable marauders, whose ravages keep a small garden in an unsightly condition. Although this chapter is devoted to a discussion hardly in accordance with the title of the book, and in no particular consequent on any of the preceding, we believe that such advice as we have to offer may not come unwelcomely to many of our readers, who would gladly avail themselves of the luxury of fresh eggs from their own hens, if they were not deterred by the fear of the annoyances to which we have alluded, and by the expectation that in the winter the chickens must be killed and cooked, in order to get any food out of them.

We should not expect much of a cow who picked up a precarious living by browzing about where there is little or nothing to be found suited to her wants; and it is not less unreasonable to expect chickens, with their voracious habits, to keep on laying eggs, unless they are in a condition to do so. Nor is the question one of mere quantity and quality of food, but of shelter; and, in short, such provisions as shall insure health and felicity.

The first requirement of health, and consequent productiveness in chickens, is freedom from the vermin that infest an old chicken-house.

Second. Proper food according to the season of the year, or, rather, the prevailing temperature.

Third. The necessary facilities for exercise, and for protection from sharp winds and cold rains when out of doors.

Fourth. Companionship and *esprit de corps* in a sufficient number of cocks and hens; for, curious as it may seem, no regular supply of eggs can be counted on from three or four chickens, however well provided for; in fact, the introduction of strangers is often found to be beneficial.

The first requirement can only be adequately met by providing two chicken-houses, which may be, if completely separated, under one roof. The chickens should

never be permitted to live in one house for more than
three weeks at a time; and, when they are turned out,
the place should be well cleaned and thoroughly white-
washed, so that at the expiration of each term a fresh,
clean house is ready to receive them.

The second requirement of food is easily provided by
giving the usual grain in summer, and in winter utilizing
the refuse of the kitchen, especially scraps of meat and
fat, potato parings, and such dainties as pigs find appetiz-
ing. In summer all the necessary animal food is provided by nature, but in winter chickens will not perform
their duty to their owners with any regularity, if unpro-
vided with carbon in some form, and a greater variety of
food than grains.

The third requirement of facilities for exercise is merely a question of space, allotted, where the chickens are not
allowed to roam at pleasure; and in this matter it is not
only desirable that the chicken-run, as it is usually called,
should be large, considering the number of chickens, but
that there should be two—one on each side of the chicken-
house—so that there may be some opportunity for nature
and man to recuperate the premises for three weeks at a
time, as in the case of the house itself. Protection from
wind and rain can be provided by building one end of the
chicken-house for a few feet above ground of brick, and
bringing down the roof-slope to form a shelter toward
the south, so that in cold or wet weather the chickens
can huddle together and keep warm without staying in

the house, and on bright winter days can bask in the sun with some reflection from the brick-work, and without being exposed to cold winds. The ground under this shelter should slope outward, so as to drain dry, and should be covered with fine gravel to aid in processes of digestion.

These various requirements, as stated, suggest a much more expensive undertaking than is at all necessary to realize them. Fig. 25 is a diagram of such a chicken-

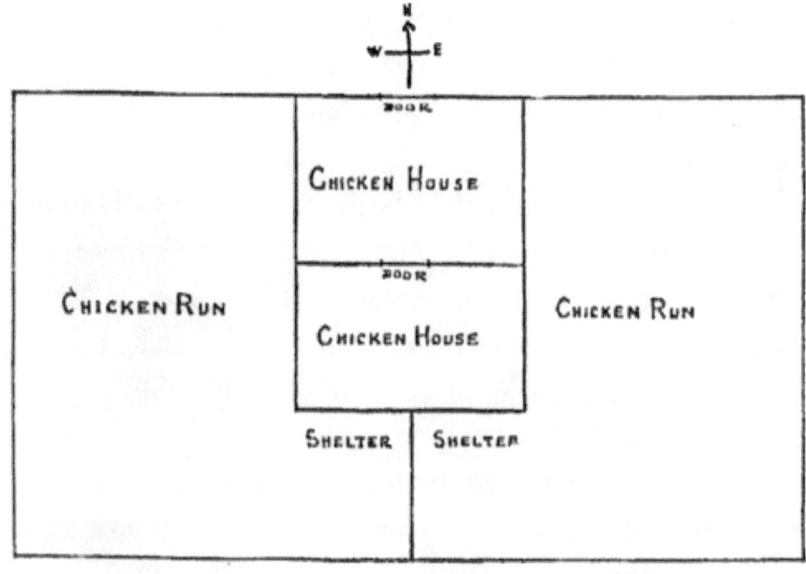

FIG. 25.

house as we would advise, the dispositions remaining the same whatever the dimensions. Fig. 26 is an external view of the same, in which we have, for the purpose of attaining some picturesque effect, added a dove-cot above, which is, however, no necessary part of the scheme as regards the chickens.

Fig. 26.

In regard to the general care of chickens, it is well to allow them to run far and wide for a time every day, because it enables them to seek out and devour the early worm, if he is foolish enough to remain near the surface, while it gives them a change of scene, and exercise that is healthful.

This daily ramble need not be a source of annoyance or a cause of damage to the garden, if it is indulged in at the proper time. The gates of the chicken-run should be opened at night after all the chickens have gone to roost, so that they may find their way out at dawn, and be easily recalled at a regular feeding-time an hour or two later, which time they learn to expect, and come running from all quarters at the first call.

In the interior of chicken-houses the necessary fittings are extremely simple, but should be constructed and disposed with due reference to the natural inclinations of the chickens and of such animals as are likely to molest them. On these and other considerations, it is well to arrange the nests, for laying on shelves so high that a tall man can just reach them to look for eggs. With these shelves one or two perches or roosting-poles may connect, and there should be enough space in front of or behind the nests for a hen to walk from end to end. The nests should be divided by partitions, but do not require to be covered, as they are, as described, sufficiently near the roof to be sheltered by it.

The necessary ties of the roof frame can be made to answer for perches or roosting-poles, and a few at right angles with these and resting upon them will generally provide ample accommodation. Mere sapling poles, such as are used for bean-poles, are *not* desirable for perches, because the bark harbors vermin in its interstices which are not easily exterminated, especially the eggs, which will hatch out in spite of cleaning and whitewashing.

A long pole sufficiently pliable to bend slightly under the weight of one chicken, and provided with small cross-sticks at regular short intervals, should be set up to form a sort of ladder escape from an aperture in the roof at the end of some perch, in order to provide a recreation for the cocks, who delight in swaying up and down on such a contrivance, which is indicated in Fig. 26. We

10

have seen as many as three cocks at one time on a spring morning disporting themselves on the same pole, and apparently acting in concert to increase the oscillations. Chickens are a good deal like other animals, including the bifurcated human species; they behave pretty well when they have everything to suit them, but when, on the contrary, they are ill housed, ill fed, and subjected to all sorts of dangers and inconveniences, they are as unhappy as we should be, similarly situated, and may be more readily excused from doing their duty, as they have, when domesticated, little or no power of bettering their condition

We have only to add to this short discussion of a large subject that a terrier dog of good ratting proclivities is a desirable accompaniment of a chicken-yard. . A dog is much better than a cat, as the dog can easily be taught to devote himself to rats, while the cat would in all probability content herself with catching chickens.

IX

REVIEW AND CONCLUSION.

ARCHITECTURAL CONSIDERATIONS IN LANDSCAPE.

THERE can be little difference of opinion as to the importance of relation between the arts of gardening and rural architecture; and we are sure that a careful consideration of all we have said under various heads will convince any one already familiar with the characteristics of architectural styles that none of the grand and affected forms of classic architecture are in keeping with the natural simplicity of landscape gardening, and that the, in one sense, more primitive forms of the domestic Gothic styles of all countries enhance the rural idea more strongly than any others. Such an old pile, for instance, as that shown in Fig. 27 has an air of being rooted and indigenous that can never be imparted to the Italian villa. Even the Swiss *chalet*, except among rocky hills where it is evident nothing very comfortable could grow, does not assume the peaceful, hospitable expression of the old gable-ended house. We can not do better than try to realize in any new structure the tone imparted to good materials by long exposure. Any attempt to bedeck our houses in varied color must result in unexpected and un-

Fig. 27.

pleasant contrast with the tones of the landscape. The natural colors of all materials are good, and we can safely employ them; but a painted house never becomes a part of our landscape. The browns and reds of bricks and tiles are always harmonious, if only because the color is a quality in them, not an application of another substance that alters their texture.

The reasons that prompt different individuals to undertake schemes of landscape improvement are as different as the results achieved. And it must be admitted that, in small undertakings at least, the achievements of those who enjoy performing some of the labor themselves, as well as paying for the labor of experts, have thus far surpassed all others, because it is not enough that a man desires a thing and is willing to pay for it; he must know enough to recognize it, even before it reaches completion in its various stages. Hawthorne says: "It has been an apothegm these five thousand years, that toil sweetens the bread it earns. For my part (speaking from hard experience, acquired while belaboring the rugged furrows of Brook Farm), I relish best the free gifts of Providence.

"Not that it can be disputed that the light toil requisite to cultivate a moderately-sized garden imparts such zest to kitchen vegetables as is never found in those of the market-gardener. Childless men, if they would know something of the bliss of paternity, should plant a seed—be it squash, bean, Indian corn, or perhaps a mere flower or worthless weed—should plant it with their own hands, and nurse it from infancy to maturity altogether by their own care. If there be not too many of them, each individual plant becomes an object of separate interest. My garden, that skirted the avenue of the manse, was of precisely the right extent. An hour or two of morning labor was all that it required. But I used to visit and revisit it a dozen times a day, and stand in deep contemplation over my vegetable progeny with a love that nobody could share or conceive of who had never taken part in the process of creation. It was one

of the most bewitching sights in the world to observe a
hill of beans thrusting aside the soil, or a row of early
peas just peeping forth sufficiently to trace a line of delicate green. Later in the season the humming-birds were
attracted by the blossoms of a peculiar kind of bean ; and
they were a joy to me, those little spiritual visitants, for
deigning to sip airy food out of my nectar cups. Multi-
tudes of bees used to bury themselves in the yellow blossoms of the summer-squashes. This, too, was a deep sat-
isfaction ; although, when they had laden themselves
with sweets, they flew away to some unknown hive,
which would give back nothing in requital of what my
garden had contributed. But I was glad thus to fling a
benefaction upon the passing breeze, with the certainty
that somebody must profit by it, and that there would be
a little more honey in the world to allay the sourness and
bitterness which mankind is always complaining of.
Yes, indeed ; my life was the sweeter for that honey."

We do not believe that it is necessary to apologize
for making so long a quotation, because our readers may
be thankful that we did not attempt to say for ourselves
what Mr. Hawthorne has told us so charmingly. Nor
shall we hesitate to cull another page of his presently
that suits our purpose, and which we hope may save our
readers many a weary line that we should otherwise
have inflicted.

In the foregoing we have often maintained the possi-
bility of so designing and planting a garden that it shall

wear its spring, its summer, its autumn, and its winter apparel effectively ; and we would only add to these remarks some considerations as to external influences upon these effects. If our planting in one direction is of such a character as to be luxuriant and dense in summer, while in winter it becomes sparse and feeble without presenting any interesting and picturesque forms of interlacing boughs, there should exist in this direction some external object or objects that may take its place and atone for the loss of effect by a new interest and enlarged perspective. Such a scene as Fig. 28 is a charming substitute for the most cheerful effects we may have created on our lawns, and, though in this picture the conditions are such as are not often realized except in mountainous country, it will serve to give a broad idea of what we mean by external conditions.

Of course, every man must to a greater or less degree put up with what falls to his share, whether of worldly goods or Nature's provisions, and we can not always find such trees as the old oak, Fig. 29, either on our own land or, what is the next best, on our neighbors.' Such an old settler is sure to look well at all seasons. When he is not " thick-leaved ambrosial," his sturdy forms will make the distance appear softer and the foreground more solid.

The dwellers in cities know little of some of the most beautiful aspects of nature, because those who are able to visit the country only do so during the summer months,

Fig. 28.

their only glimpse of the spring transitions and the late autumn changes being such as the limited resources of

Fig. 29.

the parks afford. One must live in the country to enjoy such variations as each season presents. What more beautiful than Hawthorne's description of spring:

"Some tracts in a happy exposure—as, for instance, yonder southwestern slope of an orchard, in front of that old red farmhouse—such patches of land already wear a beautiful and tender green, to which no future luxuriance can add a charm. It looks unreal—a prophecy, a hope, a transitory effect of some peculiar light which will vanish with the slightest motion of the eye.

But beauty is never a delusion ; not these verdant tracts, but the dark and barren landscape all around them, is a shadow and a dream. Each moment wins some portion of the earth from death to life ; a sudden gleam of verdure brightens along the sunny slope of a bank which an instant ago was brown and bare. You look again, and behold an apparition of green grass ! " Add to this picture our foreground of early flowering shrubs, their delicate, leafless twigs laden with many-hued blossoms, " flinging their benefactions on the passing breeze," and we feel that we shall gain little by the fulfillment of its promise in summer's less transitory realities.

In our former chapter on planting we omitted saying anything of the practical question of transplanting ; and, though we have disclaimed any intention of making this little volume more than an introduction to the study of landscape gardening, we may, without becoming deeply involved in scientific ramifications of the subject, give some advice that shall be useful to amateurs, and save them the necessity of reading and remembering much that would seem to them technical and dull.

The first question involved in successful transplantation is that of selection. The habits and appearance of trees growing in forests, surrounded by other trees, are widely different from those of trees growing in open ground. A tree, as completely as an animal, accommodates itself to its circumstances. The forest tree, being sheltered from strong and cold winds, and stayed by other trees on all sides, is not deeply or widely rooted, has thin, delicate bark, and shoots up a slender stem with few and short branches to the light and air above ; so that, when transplanted to an open lawn, it is required to change its entire mode of life, and to undergo severe hardships in battling with the weather ; the result is that it generally dies, even when the operation of transplanting has been carefully and intelligently performed. Trees growing in open ground can almost always be successfully transplanted, if the necessary precautions are observed, and the tree is not too old. The precautions consist in performing the operation at the proper season, in properly undermining the tree without injuring any of the roots, especially the more delicate ones, and in properly preparing the ground pit to receive the ball, also in the manner of filling in the soil and of watering. It is a common mistake to cut off the tops of transplanted trees, with the idea of economizing the action of the sap ; but this is as fallacious as it would be to remove one of an individual's lungs with the intention of economizing his circulation. The leaves of trees perform the necessary functions of respiration and perspiration, and those on the topmost boughs are more sensitive than others.

The best season for transplanting may vary in duration in different years, but begins when the sap has ceased to rise, and ends just before the rise has begun.

The selection being made, a sufficiently large circle should be described round the tree to include all the roots, and these should be carefully dug out with as little injury as possible, only removing as much earth from the roots as is necessary to remove the tree.

The pit should be prepared to receive the tree at least a month beforehand, should be dug larger and much deeper than is necessary to receive the ball, and should be filled in with good soil thoroughly mixed with rich manure. When the tree is transplanted, the pit should be again dug out, but now only to the necessary depth to receive the ball; the soil should then be carefully filled in, and packed so that it shall come in close contact with all the roots. If, when the spring opens, the tree does not seem to thrive, the top soil may be removed, a plenty of water poured in, and the top soil replaced. If these precautions are all taken, the transplanting of trees even thirty years old may be successfully performed.

These processes are advocated by the most eminent professors, to whose works we would refer our readers for further particulars in this as in all matters we have touched upon.

Downing's, F. L. Olmsted's, and Scott's works will be found to cover all probable contingencies, and in these works will be found exhaustive lists of trees, evergreens, shrubs, and vines, with special directions for their selection and cultivation. Any such copious information is beyond the compass of the present volume, for which we would only claim some originality in the suggestions for artistic and practical general treatment. The author was fortunate in being an assistant of Mr. Fred. Law Olmsted for three years, and has tested in practice the various methods and effects that have been the subject of these pages, in which he has tried to give a popular explanation of a professional pursuit, in the hope that the efforts of amateurs may be facilitated, and that those who desire to employ experts may not be imposed upon by unqualified persons.

11

THE END.

www.ingramcontent.com/pod-product-compliance
Lightning Source LLC
Chambersburg PA
CBHW032017010726
47493CB00007B/2453